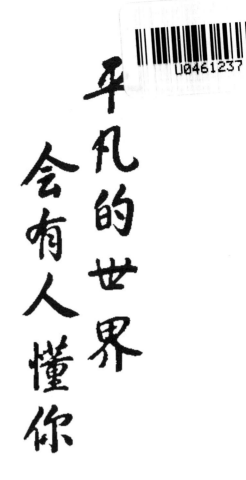

平凡的世界 会有人懂你

Blossom in Plainness, Dream in Common

SPEECHES FOR THE UNDERGRADUATES AND GRADUATES,
FROM ZHOU XUHONG DURING SERVING
AS THE PRESIDENT AT CHONGQING UNIVERSITY

周绪红任重庆大学校长期间
寄语新生和毕业生

（汉英双语版）

周绪红 著

单 宇 译

重庆大学出版社

key link of university education and the president's speech functions in educating students, promoting the spirit of university, inheriting the campus culture, and echoing the theme of the times. At the same time, the president's speeches are not only lessons for students, but also a window that connects the public and students. In recent years, the speeches made by university presidents at the opening ceremony and graduation ceremony have received wide attention from the society because the value orientations of universities behind them have been highly valued by the public. The main purpose of my speeches is to explore university education and demonstrate the spirit of the times. I try my best to make the theme clear and the content full by avoiding stereotypes and preaching, in order to further approach students, highlight spiritual connotations and remind the meaning of life; to motivate students to confront new life and challenges with confidence, calmness and courage; and to play the social role of a university through spreading positive energy and correct values to the society, making students and the public influenced and resonated.

I was among the first group of college students after the recovery of college entrance examination when more than 630,000 people in my hometown, Hunan, took part in the exam but only 3.8% of them were enrolled. Lucky as I am, I cherished much the hard-won opportunity to achieve further education. A poem "Tackling" written by Marshal Ye Jianying prevailed at that time, said, "It is tough to attack a city as well as read a book, and only hardships can overcome the obstacles in science." This poem acted as the motto written on the flyleaf of every book of mine during my university life reminding me to study hard to touch the peak of science at every moment. 40 years ago, I was luckily enrolled in university. While today, going to university has neither been an unattainable dream for most young people, nor the only way of changing their destiny. University education, in some sense, no longer equals elite education. However, facing the ever-changing world and diverse demands for talents, students and teachers are in puzzle when confronted with questions like what kinds of talents should be cultivated and how to cultivate them. I think that no matter how things change, some guidelines should remain such as the skills of study, the abilities of managing and the nature of behaving, as well as diligence, dedication and donation, pursuit of truth, integrity and innovation. Another example is the high sentiment of the country. The university life is the best period of embedding these guidelines into the minds of young people, also a key stage in the development of characters and outlooks, and a university is a vital place of acquiring knowledge and exploring the truth. Regardless of how the times changes, moral

化、呼应时代主题的重要功能。同时，校长的演讲不只是给同学们上课，也是社会观察大学和大学引领社会的窗口。近年来，大学校长在开学典礼和毕业典礼上的演讲，受到社会的广泛关注，其背后的大学价值取向被社会公众十分看重。我演讲的主要宗旨是探索大学之道与彰显时代精神，尽力做到主题明确，内容充实，避免官话套话，减少说教，贴近学生，突出精神内涵，思考人生意义，激励同学们自信、从容、勇敢地迎接新生活和新挑战，并向社会传播正能量和正确价值观以及大学的社会责任，使学生和社会受到感染并产生共鸣。

我是恢复高考后的第一届大学生，我高考那年，家乡湖南有 63 万余人报考，录取率仅 3.8%，而我成了其中的幸运儿。入学后，我倍加珍惜这来之不易的学习机会。当时流行叶剑英元帅的一首名为《攻关》的诗：“攻城不怕坚，攻书莫畏难。科学有险阻，苦战能过关。”这首诗成为我大学时代的座右铭。我把它写在几乎每一个本子、每一本书的扉页上，时时刻刻勉励自己勤奋学习、永攀科学高峰。我从上大学到如今，已经整整 40 年了。40 年后的今天，上大学对于大多数年轻人来说不再是难以企及的梦想，也不再是改变命运的唯一途径。从某些意义上来说，大学教育不再属于精英教育。但面对日新月异的世界，面对社会对人才需求的愈发多元，培养什么人、怎样培养人的问题让许多老师和学生陷入困惑。但我认为，不管世事如何变迁，总有一些“准则”是不应该改变的。譬如学习的本事、做事的本领、做人的本真；又如勤奋专注、功不唐捐；追求真理、守正创新；再如志存高远、家国情怀。而大学正是将这些“准则”埋入年轻人心田的最好时期，是砥砺品格、三观发展的关键阶段，是学习知识、探究真理的重要场所。不论时代如何变化，立德树人始终是高校教育之本，始终是大学的“初心”。如果把这些“准则”比喻为一颗颗闪亮的珍珠，这里每一篇演讲的主题就是不同的金丝线，选一根金丝线，撷几颗珍

cultivation is always the foundation and the original aspiration of college education. If you compare each guideline to a shining pearl, the themes of speeches will be different gold threads. It's a gold thread and a few pearls that constitute a beautiful necklace. The "necklace" is changing, while the original aspiration is ever-lasting.

I used to be a leader of four universities and Chongqing University is the third stop I presided, right after Chang'an University and Lanzhou University. She embraced a profound but distinctive history so that the spirit and culture "aroma" come right to your face when you walk into the campus. This book includes 14 speeches given in the opening and graduation ceremonies in my tenure, which reflects my study, understanding, appreciation and improvement of Chongqing University, particularly in cultural and talent-cultivated philosophy. No doubt that it also covers knowledge and understanding of the university spirit, the nature of education, and the concept of cultivation since I took office as a president of four universities, and reflects some of my personal views about life. My life insight, *Blossom in Plainness, Dream in Common,* is the title of this book which comes from my favorite book *World of Plainness* written by Mr. Lu Yao. Although I know that "the stupidest thing in the world is to reason young people", and even if "no one will remember what I said today in a few years", I do hope that every student in or out of college can find someone who really understands him or her.

Actually, I am very perturbed about publishing this booklet. First, most of these speeches were hurriedly drafted at the beginning or end of the semester, so there might be some errors or deficiencies. Second, in-depth thinking and researches were absent on some issues, which might lead to inevitably biased understanding or expression. Fortunately, in editing and publishing manuscripts, I was encouraged by leaders, colleagues and publishers. I am very grateful to all my colleagues who worked hard for the publication of this book, to the staff of Chongqing University Press, to the former Political Commissar of Chongqing Armed Police Corps, military calligrapher Dong Shumin for writing the title for this book, and to relevant media like *Chongqing Daily* and public support in so many years. Supposing this book was a rouser to the simplest "initial heart" of undergraduates and graduates towards study, work and life, and even a driver for those struggling people or a beacon for travelers in the night, I would be on top of the world.

Zhou Xuhong

Aug. 2018, Chongqing

珠，就能串成一条美丽的项链。变化的是"项链"，永恒的是"初心"。

我曾在四所大学担任校领导，重庆大学是继长安大学、兰州大学后，我担任校长的第三所大学。她底蕴深厚、特色鲜明，走进校园仿佛就能感受到"扑面而来"的精神和文化气息。本书收录了我任职重庆大学校长期间在开学典礼和毕业典礼上的14篇演讲稿，反映了我对重庆大学精神文化和办学理念的学习、理解、感悟和提升。当然，也包含了我在四所大学担任领导工作以来，对大学精神、教育的本质和育人理念的一些认识和理解，还折射出我个人对人生的某些思考。本书取名"平凡的世界会有人懂你"，包含了我最喜爱的书名——路遥先生的《平凡的世界》，书名本身就是我的一种人生感悟。虽然我知道，"世界上最傻的事，就是对年轻人掏心掏肺讲道理"，即便是"若干年后没有谁会记得我今天讲了什么"，但我依然期望，每一位走进或走出大学校门的孩子，都能找到真正懂自己的人。

其实，要出版这本小册子，我十分忐忑。一是这些演讲大都是在开学和期末的百忙中仓促拟就，难免存在错误或不足；二是对有些问题缺乏深入思考和研究，理解或表达难免有失偏颇。好在在书稿编辑出版过程中，得到了有关领导、同事和出版社的鼓励，使我增强了信心。我十分感谢为本书的面世做出努力的各位同事，感谢重庆大学出版社各位工作人员的辛苦工作，感谢武警重庆总队原政委、军旅书法家董书民少将为本书题写书名，感谢《重庆日报》等有关媒体和社会各界多年的支持。如果这本书能够帮助唤醒在校大学生和离开校园的毕业生对学习、对工作、对生活最简单的初心，给困顿者以力量，给夜行者以指引，于愿足矣。

周绪红

2018 年 8 月于重庆

目　录
Contents

Gathering with the Blossom of Huangge, Parting with Blossom of Life

—Speech at the 2017 Graduation Ceremony of Chongqing University

My dear students,

As the spring flowers faded, the summer lotus appeared, and when your graduate caps draw some beautiful arcs in the sky, the moment of graduating is approaching. The moment is a proof of all your perseverance, witnessing the gorgeous bloom of your colorful youth. On behalf of our university, please allow me to extend my sincere congratulations to all on your graduation and your evolution from "a fairy" to "a god" after trials and tribulations.[1]

Graduation is undoubtedly accompanied by partings. At this parting moment, don't forget to hug your classmates because you may have witnessed each other's most naive and childish moments that will become more fragrant as time goes by. Please also hug teachers who helped you along the way, though they may be a bit nagging, giving you some tricky assignments that may even trouble you overnight. All the knowledge and experience will become a rare treasure in your life.

Over the years, you might have gradually become accustomed to the life and climate here, to the spicy diet in Chongqing, to the city where you would get

---

1 It comes from the hit TV series *Eternal Love, Ten Great III of Peach Blossom*. In the series, a "Shangxian"(fairy) had to undergo all kinds of suffering before becoming a "Shangshen"(god), which is a metaphor for the students who finally graduated after four years of hard work.

聚是满园黄葛，散是缤纷四季

—— 在重庆大学 2017 届学生毕业典礼上的讲话

亲爱的同学们：

　　春花尽，夏荷起，当学位帽在蔚蓝的天空画出优美的弧线，毕业这一刻已悄然而至。这一刻，经过了你们多少日子的默然坚守；这一刻，看到了你们多彩青春的华丽绽放。让我代表学校向你们送上最衷心的祝贺，祝贺你们圆满完成学业，祝贺各位"上仙"历劫飞升"上神"[1]！

　　毕业当然也伴随着离别。在这离别的时刻，别忘了用力拥抱身边的同窗，你们可能彼此见证了对方最"傻白甜"[2]或最"呆萌萌"[3]的时光，这回忆将随时间流逝而愈觉芬芳；也请拥抱帮助你们一路走来的老师，他们或许有些唠叨，或许经常布置一些颇为"刁难"的作业让你们深夜难以入眠，可那些知识和经验都会成为你人生难得的宝藏。

1　源自当时热播的电视剧《三生三世十里桃花》，"上仙"要经历劫难才能修炼成为"上神"，比喻同学经过四年努力终于可以毕业了。
2　网络语言，形容单纯可爱的姑娘。
3　网络语言，形容憨厚可爱的小伙子。

memory because the leaves will fall in its planted season. It is not affected by seasonal changes in the outside world, and follows its own growing pace. On the campus, we can often see four seasons at the same time, when one Huangge tree is lush, the other is falling leaves or sprouting new buds. It is even more amazing that leaves burst out while some fall, presenting both green and yellow on one branch. There is no distance between life and death, so the relay of life becomes a miracle. We grew up with much praise for special plants. We love the tenacious bamboos — "they remain still no matter how strong the wind is; we praised the evergreen pinetrees — "the unyielding pine trees will not bow to the changing time"; we appreciate the erecting poplar trees — "they stay towering and uncompromising in the sky". However, few have set their sights on Huangge trees that are distinctively wonderful. I praise them for their "toughness and tenacity", and more for they "maintain the rhythm, keep the true nature, and stay calm for the whole life". Huangge is the city tree of Chongqing, symbolizing diligence, bravery and tenacity of Chongqing people, and we must face this rapid changing era just like Huangge trees.

Keep your own pace like Huangge trees in a hurry world.

Many people hold the idea that this is a "fast" era. When going out, we choose the fastest means of transportation; when reading and studying, we hope to circle the main points as soon as possible. We are often devoured by anxiety, feared of frustration, and hungry for shortcuts. We only hope that we can reach the pinnacle of life at the fastest speed at a young age. And life does give us reasons for anxiety: job hunting, house buying, marriage getting, old caring... all kinds of worries are overwhelming us all the time. A recent survey by *People's Tribune* found that more than 60% of those surveyed think that they are highly anxious, and 89% of them agree that "anxiety for all people" has become a common issue in China.

In fact, every stage of life deserves our savouring, which is just like that in the four seasons, we can enjoy different sceneries during our lifetime. Looking back on college time, it is certainly an unforgettable moment to receive recognition and applause from the podium, but I also appreciate the students walking towards the library and study rooms with their books regardless of severe winter or midsummer. Spreading youthful enthusiasm on the stage and the stadium is also certainly a memory worthy of cherishing, and I also appreciate the students who are obscured but hard-working in the laboratory. Recently, I believe that every student has been inspired by the news reporting that Chongqing University takes the lead in designing

什么季节落叶，不因外界时令的变化，不畏秋风扫落叶，自有自的节奏。我们常常在校园里看到"四季同框"的景象，这棵黄葛树正郁郁葱葱，而那棵正在落叶飘零，旁边一棵却在吐露新芽。甚为奇妙的是，黄葛树一边落叶又一边生出新叶，鹅黄嫩绿同现枝条，生死相连没有距离，生命的接力成为奇迹。从小到大，我们赞美过太多的植物。我们爱"竹"的坚韧，"千磨万击还坚劲，任尔东西南北风"；我们赞"松"的长青，"不以时迁者，松柏也"；我们敬"杨"的挺拔，"参天耸立，不折不挠"。然而，少有人将目光投到黄葛树上。但黄葛树自有它的精彩，我赞美它"坚韧顽强"，更赞美它"保持节奏，坚守本色，从容笃定"。黄葛树是重庆的市树，它象征着重庆人民勤奋、勇敢、顽强的精神品质，我们要像黄葛树一样面对这个飞速发展的时代。

这个时代或许有些"焦急"，要像黄葛树那样活出自己的节奏。

很多人说，这是一个"快"时代。出门远行时，我们选择最快的交通工具；读书求知时，我们希望最快圈出要点。我们经常满怀焦虑、害怕挫折、寻求捷径，只希望年纪轻轻就以最快的速度走上人生巅峰。而生活也确实给了我们焦虑的理由：求职、买房、婚姻、养老……种种愁绪"才下眉头，却上心头"。《人民论坛》最近一项调查发现，超过六成人认为自己的焦虑程度较高，89%的人认同"全民焦虑"已成为当下中国的社会通病。

事实上，人生的每个阶段都值得我们细细品味，正如一年四季，人生时时有风景。回顾大学时光，登上领奖台接受表彰和喝彩当然是难忘的时刻，但我也同样欣赏同学们夹着书冒着严寒或酷暑走向图书馆、自习室的身影；在万众瞩目的舞台和赛场上挥洒青春热情当然是值得珍藏的回忆，但我也同样欣赏在实验室里默默无闻却勤奋努力的你。最近，相信每个重大人都被一则新闻所振奋，"重庆大学牵头设

leisurely song of separation gradually sounded in my ears, thousands of words cannot express my feeling. I hope that after going through thousands of sails, you are still the youngest. I wish all of you a gathering with the blossom of Huangge, a parting with blossom of life.

Thank you all!

静；你们是天空中洁白的云，永远倒映在母校的波心。"千川江海阔，风好正扬帆"，当悠悠的离歌在耳畔渐渐响起，千言万语道不尽珍重，愿你们历尽千帆，归来仍是如初少年；愿你们聚是满园黄葛，散是缤纷四季！

谢谢大家！

Don't Disappoint the Youth

—Speech at the Opening Ceremony of 2017 Undergraduates of Chongqing University

Dear students,

Good morning!

In this lovely season of harvest and hope, we get together by Jinyun Lake to witness your opening new journey of life. You have brought vitality and vigor to the campus. Welcome to be a significant member in Chongqing University! Besides, on today's 33rd Teachers' Day in China and on behalf of the school, I would like to extend my greetings and respect to the teachers who will accompany you on your new journey!

My dear students, the intersection of university and youth marks a crucial moment in life. For this moment, you have shown the indomitable determination and courage to the world. After a dozen years of hard-working study, you are finally rewarded by fate. Now that you have realized your dreams and come into the long-awaited university, I wish that you could brighten up a better future with your youth.

My dear students, a university is a hall of education. In order to achieve the integration of knowledge and life, our university cultivates the persistent pursuit of the scientific and humanistic spirit, the moral consciousness of acting and the inner peace and tranquility. At this moment, the campus is a fertile ground for your enrichment of knowledge and personality, a melting pot for sharpening your soul and mind, and a paradise for cherishing youth and friendship. In the future, she

莫让芳华负朝夕

—— 在重庆大学 2017 级本科生开学典礼上的讲话

亲爱的同学们：

上午好！

山城九月，秋色宜人。在这个满载收获和希望的季节，我们齐聚在缙云湖畔，共同见证你们踏入人生的全新旅程。你们的到来，为校园带来了蓬勃的生机和朝气。欢迎你们成为重大的一员！今天也是我国第 33 个教师节，在此，我谨代表学校，向即将陪伴你们继续前行的老师们，致以节日的问候和崇高的敬意！

同学们，大学与青春的交汇，是人生中至关重要的时刻。为了这一时刻的到来，你们向世人展示了义无反顾的决心和一往无前的勇气，历经十年寒窗磨砺，终获命运的褒奖。如今你们心愿遂成，走进了向往已久的大学校园，我期待你们用青春点亮更美好的未来。

同学们，大学是育人的殿堂。为了实现知识与生命的融合，这里涵育的是对科学精神和人文精神的执着追求，做人行事的道德自觉以及内心的沉潜宁静。在当下，她是你们增长学识、完善人格的沃土，

will become the cornerstone of your career and the source of motivation for your pursuing a happy life. It is on your best time that you come to Chongqing University, and I hope to see you rambling together under the Huangge trees, surfing in the sea of books, enlightening your mind in the dialogue with the masters, enriching yourselves by practice and thinking, and trying to find answers about life and ideals when hugging the morning glow and seeing the sun set off.

Liu Qing, a famous writer, once said that throughout the long road of life only a few steps really matter, especially those in one's youth. University time is the brightest season and the most important step in your life. You have strong impulses flowing in your body, and longings for freedom just like a poem line goes that "eagles soar in the sky, fishes swim in the river, and all kinds of creatures contend for freedom". You are passionate for the world and curious about all new things. How can you live up to this great time and turn your youthful expectations into unparalleled moments in life? This is another question you need to answer today.

My dear students, youth is not always a bed of roses. You must learn to persevere while passing through the thorns. When you start college life full of confidence, the fate will first make a joke with you: you will find that after only one summer vacation, your excellence will eclipse among the new partners. In the classroom, you may be no longer the focus of others; in the race, you might be no longer the leader in front; in the community, you will not be the backbone of the members anymore; even after exams, you are no longer so confident. A great many talented and competitive peers in the university along with heavier study tasks put you under great pressure in the face of great challenges and fierce competitions. The road ahead may be more difficult, but it also offers you a good opportunity to practice and improve. You have to learn to face it with greater perseverance, which means that you should never give up the original aspirations and beliefs in times of difficulties, entertaining the desire for success in the time of frustrations and insisting on the goals and ideals of life after failure. Only by perseverance can you steer the sail of growth and become stronger and mature.

The struggling history of Chongqing University for nearly a century is the best interpretation of adherence. From the creation of a "complete and profound university" to today's "establishing the reputation of the university in Southwest and creating a first-class university", generations of CQUers have adhered to setting moral integrity and giving helping hands. They have assumed the responsibility of

是提升心志、磨砺灵魂的熔炉，是释放青春、收获友谊的乐园。在未来，她将成为你们事业起步的累土基石、追求幸福生活的动力源泉。来到重大，正值你们最好的年华，我希望看见你们在黄葛树下结伴同行，在书籍的海洋中游历四方，在与大师的对话中启迪心智，在实践和思辨中充实自我、历练身心，在拥抱朝霞和送别夕阳中，找寻到关于人生、关于理想、关于生活的答案。

著名作家柳青说过，人生的道路虽然漫长，但紧要处常常只有几步，特别是当人年轻的时候。大学时光是你们生命中最灿烂的季节，也是你们人生道路上最紧要的一步。你们的身体里涌动着强烈的力量，内心渴望着"鹰击长空，鱼翔浅底，万类霜天竞自由"；你们对世界葆有炽热的情感，对于一切新鲜事物都充满了好奇。如何不负这大好时光？如何将年轻时的期许转化为生命中无与伦比的精彩？这是你们今天需要面对的又一人生考题。

同学们，青春并不总是鲜花遍地，你们要在穿越荆棘中学会坚守。当你满怀信心地开始大学生活，命运首先会与你开个不大不小的玩笑：你会发现，仅仅过了一个暑假，你的优秀就湮没在同样优秀的新伙伴中。课堂里，你不再是大家关注的焦点；赛道上，你不再是一马当先的领跑者；社团中，你不再是当仁不让的主心骨；甚至考试后，你都不再那么信心十足、胜券在握。大学里人才济济、强手如林，再加上繁重的学习任务，会使你承受很大的压力，面临极大的挑战，遭遇激烈的竞争。今后的道路，可能会更加坎坷难行，但这是你锻炼成长的好机遇，你要学会面对、学会坚守。所谓坚守，就是在困难面前永不放弃初心和信仰，挫折之中始终饱含着对成功的渴望，失败以后愈加坚定人生的目标和理想。只有学会坚守，你才能掌控住成长的风帆，愈挫弥坚，驶向成熟。

重大近一个世纪的奋斗历史，便是对坚守最好的诠释和注解。从

he finally harvested academic fruits.

My dear students, there are countless choices lying ahead in the future and you are required to be wise, careful and decisive enough when you make a decision. Just like Sun Xiaowen and Gui Yin'gang who focused on growing into better selves and stepping into better lives, you should "insist on pursuing by the means of innovation"[1] to live life to the full. Please remember that the choices you make today determine your future. Mr. Ye Shengtao, an educator, once said, "The ease in youth is a draft in old, and the greatest sorrow in life is no more than disappointing your youth." Although you have just entered school, and you still cannot prepare a plan for life completely, in my opinion, tapping your true love deep in your heart, looking for your own true qualities, and positioning for the style of college life are the foundation to complete the transformation of sublimation in life. In this regard, I have a few suggestions I want to share with you.

First of all, I hope you can take books as your friends and improve yourselves continuously. Books are to life as lyrics are to music and sunlight to the earth. In the era without the Internet, reading was a journey through time and space that made people available to the scenery of history or the lifetime of historical figures in the spiritual world. Today, with the explosion of information, books, as the crystallization of human thought and wisdom, have also become the spiritual foundation for universities to uphold academics, seek truth, and enhance the realm. "What do we want from reading? It makes us rational." Western philosopher Bacon believed that "Histories make men wise; poets witty; the mathematics subtle; natural philosophy deep; moral grave; logic and rhetoric able to contend." In ancient times, "If the scholar-official did not read for three days, he might not remember the doctrine of truth, and he looked abominable when looking in the mirror, and his words didn't make any sense." The biggest reason for reading today is to shield the gloss, to get rid of the mediocrity, to refine your temperament, to obtain the inner sedimentation and tranquility, and to discover the beauty of the world. "One who is filled with knowledge always behaves with elegance." Although reading can't stop the passing of time, by the means of reading, people can reshape their knowledge structure, construct their value judgments, cultivate aesthetic habits,

---

1   It comes from "Asking for Dajun Fu" by Liu Yuxi, a literary scholar of the Tang Dynasty. It means persistent pursuit and innovation.

的研究并取得了一系列重要成果。为了追寻心中所爱，桂银刚选择了遵从内心的声音，加之刻苦付出，终于迎来了学术的春天。

同学们，你们的未来要面临无数次的选择，每一次选择的背后，都需要开启智慧、缜密思考、从容决断。要像孙小雯和桂银刚那样，将目光着眼于更好的自己和更好的生活，"以不息为体，以日新为道"[1]，在不断的取舍中，为自己增加生命的内涵与厚度。请记住，你们今天的选择，最终将决定明天的模样。教育家叶圣陶先生说过，"少年时期的放浪是晚年的汇票，人生的最大悲痛莫过于辜负青春"。虽然刚刚进校的你们，还无法形成完整的人生规划，但在我看来，挖掘你们内心深处真实的热爱、寻找你们自己真正的特质，为大学生活的格调定位，是今后完成人生蜕变和升华的基础。对此，我有几点体会与你们分享。

首先，希望你们与书籍为友，不断完善自我。书籍之于生命，如同乐谱之于音乐，阳光之于大地。在没有互联网的时代，读书就是一场说走就走的时空旅行，让人们在精神世界里或饱览历史长河的风光，或凝望历史人物的一生。在信息爆炸的今天，书籍作为人类思想与智慧的结晶，同样成为大学崇尚学术、探求真理、提升境界的精神根基。"读书何所求？将以通事理。"西方哲人培根认为，"读史使人明智，读诗使人灵秀，数学使人周密，科学使人深刻，伦理学使人庄重，逻辑修辞使人善辩"。古时"士大夫三日不读书，则义理不交于胸中，对镜觉面目可憎，向人亦语言无味"。今日读书的最大理由就是在与书籍的相守中屏蔽浮华、摆脱平庸、提升气质，由此获得内心的沉淀和宁静，发现世间的美丽。"腹有诗书气自华"，读书虽不能阻止时间的流逝，但人们可以通过读书改善自己的知识构成，构建价值

---

1 出自唐代文学家，哲学家刘禹锡的《问大钧赋》。体，准则；道，法则。意思是坚持追求，坚持创新。

expand and extend the limited length of life. Read more classics for the classics have stood the test and screening of time and they are the accretion of the times and the crystallization of culture. By reading the classics, we could accept the influence of traditional culture, feel the thoughts of the sages, sublimate our soul, and make our soul keep up with the pace of walking. Read more books to broaden your horizon, overcome obstacles of thinking, stimulate potential energy and passion for creativity, trigger the desire for independent thinking, and form unique cognitions and views from questioning, criticism, and inheritance. As Roman Rowland said, "Never has there been anyone who studies for the sake of study except that he studies to read himself, explore himself and examine himself."

Secondly, I hope that you could befriend practice and constantly measure yourselves. There is an expression to describe the university called "ivory tower", and some people understand it as "a detached society of the new world which is separated from the real world". But in reality, the university and society are inseparable and tightly connected. We have recognized this point and try to make changes. Today, Chongqing University not only provides you with a sound and favorable study environment, but also an increasing number of innovation practice bases including the social practice internship bases, the college students' innovation and entrepreneurship bases, and the student communities; you must take the initiative to devote yourselves to the complex class of social practice to temper yourself and improve professional skills through which you understand the society, test yourselves, and realize self-values. As you can see, neither the society nor the country is perfect. But we do not have to blame others, let alone indulge in vulgarity. We have the responsibility to make changes. When we are together, we are like drops of water merging into another drops or beams of light embracing other beams of light. Only by lighting up ourselves can we have a bright future. Only by clustering together can we illuminate the future of our country. Six undergraduates enrolled in 2013 majored in broadcasting and hosting including Gu Chengxin, Ren Zhijun and Xing Zekun established the "Sound Seeking Volunteer Association". They constantly send free recorded stories and children's poems to the left-behind children in the mountainous regions with their footprints reaching all over Chongqing's mountainous primary schools, and some volunteer activities such as "Sound Seeking for Dreams" and "Good Night Baby" cared for more than 3,000 left-behind children with kindness. At present, the number of volunteers in the team has grown from

判断，培育审美习惯，让生命的有限疆域得以拓展和延伸。要多读经典，因为经典作品经受了岁月的考验与筛选，它们是时代的沉淀和文化的结晶。通过阅读经典，接受传统文化熏陶，感受先贤的思想，升华自己的灵魂，让你的灵魂跟上行走的脚步。要博览群书，通过广泛涉猎打破视野的局限，克服思维的障碍，激发自己内在的能量与创造的激情，触发独立思考的欲望，在质疑、批判和继承中形成独树一帜的认知和观点。正如罗曼·罗兰所说，"从来没有人为了读书而读书，只有在书中读自己，在书中发现自己，或检查自己"。

其次，希望你们与实践为友，不断考量自我。有个形容大学的词叫"象牙塔"，有人把它理解为"超脱现实社会、远离生活之外的天地"，但是，现实中的大学与社会是密不可分、紧紧相连的。我们已经认识到了这一点，并开始做出改变。今天的重大，不仅为你们提供了一张安静的书桌、一座堂皇的图书馆，还有越来越多的创新实践基地、社会实践实习基地、大学生创新创业基地、学生活动社团供你们选择；你们要主动投身于社会实践这个大课堂，淬火锤炼，增长本领，在实践中认识社会、检验自己、实现价值。我们已经看到，社会并不完美，国家也有不足，但我们无须怨天尤人，更不能沉溺于低俗，我们有责任去改变。我们在一起，就像一滴水融入另一滴水，就像一束光簇拥着另一束光，唯有点亮自己，才有美好前程；唯有簇拥在一起，才能照亮国家的未来。我校播音与主持艺术专业的顾成鑫、任志骏、幸泽坤等6名2013级本科生，立足专业特长成立了"寻声志愿者协会"，定期将录制好的故事和童诗免费赠送给山区留守儿童，他们的足迹已经遍布重庆山区小学，"寻声有梦""宝贝晚安"等活动温暖了3 000余名留守儿童。目前，"寻声"志愿者队伍从50余人壮大到几万人，参与录制的志愿者有敬一丹、赵普、徐涛等知名播音主持人及社会各界爱心人士。他们还尝试自主创业，在重庆设立了首个

and strictly demand yourselves with rigorous discipline, determined will, and regular living style to lay the foundation for study and life in the future. From now on, every day you spend in Chongqing University will be the unforgettable memories of youth. The memories of these years will be like a gorgeous picture scroll shining with dazzling brilliance, and also like a sparkling meteor flashing away. But I believe that after years of sharpening and practicing in university, you will definitely achieve your own excellence.

Dear students, please pack up your bag and live up to your youth!

Thank you all!

一天，都是青春的记忆，这几年的记忆会像一幅绚丽的画卷，光彩夺目；又如天上的流星，一闪而过。但我相信，经过岁月的磨砺，经过重大的洗礼，你们定能收获属于自己的精彩！

　　同学们，背上追梦的行囊启程吧，莫让芳华负朝夕！

　　谢谢大家！

Focus Makes the Future

—Speech at the Opening Ceremony of 2017 Graduate Students of Chongqing University

Dear students,

Good morning!

Nice to meet you here. You have brought happiness and energy to this university in these days. Here, on behalf of all the teachers and students of Chongqing University, I would like to express my sincere welcome to you all!

My dear students, studying as graduate students is different from that of undergraduates. You are no longer just passive receivers of knowledge. Instead, you will become explorers of natural laws and discoverers of cultural mysteries. Academic research in university is a major training method for postgraduate students, and it may become a starter for your academic research career. It can be said that doing academic research is the process of focusing on, analyzing, and solving problems. It not only requires you to be diligent and intelligent, creative and reflective, but also depends on your persistent and consistent "focus", a familiar word to us. In childhood, teachers told us the story of "cat fishing" and taught us to "focus on one thing". In fact, "focus" has always been mentioned in our life. Today, I want to talk about focusing on studies.

First of all, it is necessary to concentrate your mind so as to lay the foundation for success.

As an ancient precept goes, "Do not ask widely, and then you can acquire the

专注以致远

—— 在重庆大学 2017 级研究生开学典礼上的讲话

亲爱的同学们：

大家上午好！

很高兴在重大与你们相见。因为你们的到来，这几天校园里到处洋溢着青春的气息，充满着喜悦的气氛。在此，我代表重庆大学全体师生员工欢迎你们！

同学们，研究生阶段的学习不同于本科，你们不再只是知识的被动接受者，而将成为自然规律的探索者和文化奥秘的发现者。学术研究是研究生培养的一种主要方法，你们当中一部分人的学术研究生涯或许就从这里起步。可以说，学术研究就是聚焦问题、分析问题、解决问题的过程，不但需要你们勤于思考、勇于创新、敢于反思，更有赖于你们要保有持之以恒的专注。说到"专注"，我们并不陌生。在孩童时代，师长就给我们讲过"小猫钓鱼"的故事，教导我们要"全神贯注，专心致志"。实际上，"专注"一直与我们的人生相伴。今天，我想给大家谈谈做学问也需要"专注"。

authorized four invention patents, and won more than ten honorary awards at all levels. Being the only student member who participated in the formulation of relevant international technical standards, he said, "The heavy scientific research has not annoyed me. Instead, it has stimulated my enthusiasm for progress." Xiao Song found his interest in scientific research. In his world, researching itself has become a kind of happiness.

Along the way of academic research, there are always bumps and barriers, but they cannot prevent us from getting happiness. As long as you concentrate on study, eliminate some interference, devote yourself to study and actively strive for progress, you will not feel exhausted. Unlike the acquisition of money and material, the joy of study is the satisfaction after painstaking efforts to reveal the truth. "The thing you're committed to will definitely bring you success." As long as we maintain sufficient focus and continuous investment, the biggest beneficiary of study is ultimately ourselves.

Thirdly, we must stay focused in the hustle and bustle of the world and stick to our inner peace.

Although we study on campus, it is undeniable that "the outside world is wonderful". The ancients said, "If you want more, you may lose your heart. Once you lost your heart, you may lose your goal, and finally lose your mind in a further way." Affected by the negative influence of society, people are losing their ability to concentrate. "Concentrating on reading" and "leading a quiet life" become impossible. We spend too much time on mobile phones and less time on study and research. Some people are obsessed with fragmented reading, and they are eager to be quick. They just want to enjoy ready-made answers from the Internet search. In the end, they may acquire knowledge superficially, and then become confused. Some people are eager for immediate benefits and various "hot spots" and change their research direction at will. They produce many so-called "research results" and show them to others; some people even take a risk violating the academic ethics, as a result of which academic misconduct happens from time to time.

Facing the faster pace of life, the innovation of information technology, the impact of multiculturalism, and the complexity and change of society, focus is the bottom line for us to keep the creed of mind in life. It will help us eliminate misunderstandings and maintain the inner peace in our heart. Xian Xuefu, professor of mining engineering in our school is a well-known expert in mine safety technology

着如一，也是克服挫折的一剂良药。专注做学问的过程本身就是探索真理、追求完美的过程，一开始觉得它有多么枯燥，一旦你专注投入，取得学术上的进步，就会感受到无限的乐趣。电气工程学院2016届博士毕业生肖淞，在校期间发表了高水平学术论文5篇，授权发明专利4项，获得各级荣誉奖10余项，被授予中法双博士学位，还作为仅有的学生成员，参与制定了相关国际技术标准。他说："繁重的科研工作没有让我产生厌烦，反而越发地激发我前进的热情。"肖淞在科研中发现了自己的热爱，在他的世界里，专注做学问，本身已经成为一种幸福。

学术研究从来就没有平坦的道路可走，往往会遭遇失败、面临困境，但不能阻止我们从中获得快乐。专心致志地做学问，排除或放弃其他干扰之事，全身心地投入学习并积极地争取进步，这样你的心里就不会感到筋疲力尽。不同于金钱和物质的获取，做学问的快乐，是呕心沥血揭示真理后的满足，是绞尽脑汁攻克难关后的酣畅。"凡是专精于一，必有动人之处"，只要保持足够专注和持续投入，做学问的最大受益者终是我们自己。

第三，要在世间喧嚣里保持专注，坚守内心的平静。

虽然我们在校园里学习，但不可否认"外面的世界很精彩"。古人云："欲多则心散，心散则志衰，志衰则思不达。"受社会的不良影响，人们正在丧失专注的能力，让"潜心读书"和"宁静致远"变得不那么容易。我们花费太多的时间在看手机上，而在学习、研究上花的时间越来越少。有的人痴迷于碎片化的阅读，一心求快，只想从网络搜索中享用现成的答案，到头来蜻蜓点水、浅尝辄止，或者眼花缭乱、无所适从。有的人贪求立竿见影的收益，热衷于追逐各种"热点"，随意改变研究方向，快出、多出"成果"以示人；还有的人不惜铤而走险，触碰学术道德的红线，以致学术不端行为时有发生。

in China and a pioneer of basic research on coalbed methane. Professor Xian only gives himself four days off a year and devoted himself to the research work of coalbed methane theory and its engineering application in the rest of time. Professor Xian has adhered to the responsibilities of scholars and defended the academic dignity for decades; from this "boring" work, he has achieved a fulfilling life with real concentration.

When the world becomes impetuous, it doesn't mean that you have a reason to follow the wave. Due to your concentration, you may seem to be "incompatible" with others, or even "dumb", but all of those will allow you to stand at a height that others can't reach and make lots of achievements. The calmness of "keeping still no matter how strong the wind is" can never be understood by those who are out of patience.

My dear students, a new life is about to begin. A singer named Luciano Pavarotti once asked his father when he graduated from a normal university, "Should I be a teacher or a singer?" His father replied, "If you want to sit on two chairs, you may fall from the middle of the chairs. Life allows you to choose only one chair to sit on." Luciano Pavarotti chose a chair and later became a superstar in the world of music. Focus lies on persistence and confidence, and it is focus that makes you go further. I hope that you will establish a clear and lasting goal, determine the strength of perseverance and patience, hold on the direction of your own progress and don't give up; as postgraduate students, try to focus on study and shaping yourselves, and make concentration as your daily habits, build your own future in dedication, and contribute your wisdom to building Chongqing University into a world-class university and to the great rejuvenation of the Chinese nation.

Thank you all!

当面对生活节奏的加快、信息技术的革新、多元文化的冲击、社会复杂多变等诸多考验时，专注就是坚守底线、抱元守一的人生信条，帮助我们排除杂念，维系宁静。我校采矿工程学科的教授、与重大同龄的鲜学福院士，是我国著名矿山安全技术专家、煤层气基础研究的开拓者。鲜院士基本上一年只给自己放四天假，其余时间都致力于矿井煤层气理论及其工程应用的研究工作。鲜院士以数十年如一日的坚持，恪守着学者的本分，捍卫着学术的尊严，在这看似枯燥的工作里，用真正的专注获得了充实的人生。

当世界开始浮躁，并不意味着你们就有理由随波逐流。由于专注，你可能看起来与旁人有些"格格不入"，甚至会显得有些"呆傻"，但正是这种"格格不入"和"呆傻"，才能让你站到别人难以企及的高处，收获丰硕的成果。"千磨万击还坚劲，任尔东西南北风"的从容，是那些太过急功近利的人永远都无法领会到的。

同学们，新的生活即将开启。歌唱家鲁契亚诺·帕瓦罗蒂从师范大学毕业时，请教他的父亲："我是当教师呢，还是做歌唱家？"其父回答说："如果你想同时坐在两把椅子上，你可能会从椅子中间掉下去。生活要求你只能选一把椅子坐上去。"鲁契亚诺·帕瓦罗蒂选了一把椅子，后来成为世界歌坛的超级巨星。专注贵在专一，专注贵在执着，专注贵在自信，专注才能致远。我希望同学们树立清晰而恒久的目标，笃信坚持和耐心的力量，认定自己前进的方向，矢志不渝，永不言弃；在研究生学习阶段专注于学问，专注于做人，让专注融入日常成为习惯，在专注中成就自己的未来，为把重庆大学建设成世界一流大学奉献才智，为实现中华民族的伟大复兴贡献力量。

谢谢大家！

and not to be burdened by being perfect. Making some choices is accompanied by abandoning other choices, which means that choosing one path means giving up all other paths. There is no standard answer to the choice of life, just following your own heart. The process of continuous self-selection is the process of making yourself the best.

To make good choices, we need concentration.

When we were young, teachers told us a ridiculous story about "pulling up the seedlings to help them grow". However, when we grow up, we often make such mistakes. As soon as you have a direction, you want to achieve something. Otherwise you will be confused and suffered in dilemma. This is a common mistake for people in their twenties. However, to improve your life, being utilitarian and impetuous is of no use when accumulation is really in need. Although hard work matters, making choices sometimes can be more important. But please keep in mind that after making a choice, there are still a long way to go. You have to make unprecedented efforts to prove your choice. You are at the age of struggle, so do not choose ease. It is no doubt that the breeze will come for you when you are in full bloom. Recently, craftsmanship spirit has been constantly reported by media. I think, no matter what kind of business you are going to do in the future, you must calm down and feel the serenity of the craftsman in the deep heart.

My dear students, a bright future is waiting ahead. Having a cup of tea and a scroll of book beside you, you can feel the tranquility of "not being disturbed by anyone", or you can judge the current situation and work hard, enjoying the freedom of "appreciating all attracting scenery in one day". And I would like to give you advice that whenever you make the choice, stay true to your original aspirations.

My dear students, the sorrow of separating is beyond expression. It is time to say goodbye, but I know that at the moment you make a happy turn, your alma mater will pray for you in your lifetime; I know that no matter how long the time is, the alma mater always understands your sadness and joy! Today, we say goodbye to each other and I hope that in the future, you will be relieved for that all kinds of choices and thousands of paths will not disappoint your life!

Thank you all!

化无全功，巧其音者拙其羽，丰其实者啬其花。"每个人都有自己的优势和劣势，"役其所长，则事无废功；避其所短，则世无弃材矣"，扬长避短是人生的一大哲学。我们必须学会做人生的减法，不要为"全"字所累。有选择就会有放弃，选择了一条路就意味着放弃了其他所有的路。人生的选择并没有标准答案，只要你的选择是遵从自己的内心，不断自我选择的过程就是使自己成为最好的自己的过程。

做好选择，我们更需要一些定力。

小时候老师就给我们讲过"揠苗助长"的故事，告诉我们这很荒唐，长大后，我们却时常犯这样的错误。刚有了方向，就想有结果，不然就陷入迷茫、痛苦、挣扎，这是二十几岁的年轻人常常走入的误区。但是，完善人生不能急功近利、心浮气躁，而需要沉淀和积累。选择固然重要，有时可能比努力更重要，但是别忘了选择之后，还有千山万水要跨越。你必须比任何时候都要更加努力，才能证明你的选择是正确的。你们处于奋斗的年龄，不要选择安逸。我们"面向太阳，不问花开"，坚信"你若盛开，清风自来"。最近，媒体常常在描述一个词叫作"工匠精神"。我想，不论你们接下来要进入的是哪行哪业，都要静下心来体悟手艺人安静而安定的内心，体会什么叫"简约深美"。

同学们，等待你们的将是更为广阔的天地。未来的生活，你们可以一杯茶、一卷书，感悟"心远地自偏"的宁静，也可以审时势、敢打拼，享受"一日看尽长安花"的潇洒。而我，只愿你们，在做任何选择时，都不曾忘记今日在这风雨操场把握的初心。

同学们，道不尽的是离愁，说不完的是别殇。就要说再见了，可我知道，你们幸福转身的一瞬，是母校为你们驻足凝眸的一生；我更知道，无论时光多么久远，母校永远知你冷暖，懂你悲欢！今日，我们挥手作别，只望他日，你们都能欣慰，种种选择，千般道路，此生不负！

谢谢大家！

wonderful time in life. Time in university flies. You must seize this golden period of life to reasonably arrange every day and hour of university life, make full use of the high-quality resources provided by the school, and study with a sense of urgency. We should achieve both humanistic literacy and scientific spirit.

I sincerely wish you a perfect personality, outstanding academic performance, and true happiness in the four years to come!

My dear students, the military training will follow the opening ceremony, in which you will learn the concepts of strict discipline, hardworking style, perseverance and determination to win the battle. This is another wealth that will benefit you for the lifetime. Here, let's pay tribute to our loveliest PLA officers.

My dear students, a line goes that "The roc rises with the wind, soaring up nine miles in a day." I believe that Chongqing University is a university where you can achieve your ambition and make down-to-earth practice and also a university that can stimulate your youth to create your own wonders. Please embrace your beautiful dreams and set off! I wish all the students full of energy every day at Chongqing University!

Thank you all!

能打胜仗的决心，这又是一笔获益终身的财富。在这里，让我们向最可爱的解放军官兵致敬！

同学们，"大鹏一日同风起，扶摇直上九万里。"我相信，重大是能让你们志存高远、躬行实干的大学，也是能让你们激扬青春、创造精彩的大学。怀抱好你们美好的梦想，出发吧！祝同学们在重大的每天都充满力量！

谢谢大家！

you're successful as long as you live and study making full use of your energy and abtainable resources. It is precisely because of such different successes that constitute the rich lives and the colorful world. Perhaps we are all "farsighted", always living in looking up at others, and ignoring the happiness around us. I want to tell you that we are all ordinary people, because we are all from the "ordinary world", but we can all succeed, as long as we strive to do our best in our worlds, do every ordinary thing around us well.

As a graduate of Chongqing University, it is also true that you may not all become so-called "elites" in society, but I believe that even if you are ordinary members of society, you are also backbones for propelling the movement of society. Today, you are seeds scattered throughout society, taking your roots and thriving in your ordinary worlds; as Lu Yao said, "I want to live a realistic life. However, sometimes, I would like to jump out from the real life and peep on the platform named dream", in realizing self-value and fulfilling family and social responsibilities, gathering the power of countless "ordinary people" thereby promoting social development, national rejuvenation and the prosperity of a country, as CQUers, we should shoulder the social responsibility of "rejuvenating the nation and vowing to be the striker". In the future, whether you are going to be a designer, a host, a judge, or a soldier ..., your hard work is the "pushing hands" of this era! Although you are in a world of plainness, there must be someone understanding you!

We long for achievement but we must accept plainness which is more normal in life. In the torrent of progress of the times, it is not easy to go up, and harder to let it go. In this era of rapid information development, the entrepreneurial story of Ma Huateng[1], the full passion of Steve Jobs that "we are here to put a dent in the universe" and some so-called "successful studies" that surround us through the Internet showed us the mirages of "success" which seem so close and easy to touch. But in this world, not all "reasonable" and "beautiful" things can exist or be realized as you wish. The whole society will be proud of you for your great achievements; your families, friends and the society will as well applaud you if you lead a happy life though without accomplishments, staying true and striving to be better, rather than looking up in the glory of others. The modern poet Bian Zhilin once said, " You stand on the bridge viewing the sight; You're beheld by the viewer from height." Much of

---

1   Also known as Pony Ma, is the founder, chairman and CEO of Tencent, one of the most valuable companies in Asia.

Study Calls for Craftsmanship Spirit

—Speech at the Opening Ceremony of 2016 Graduate Students of Chongqing University

Dear students,

Good morning!

In this lovely and cool early autumn, Chongqing University welcomed 4,700 new graduate students. First of all, on behalf of the university, I would like to extend a warm welcome to you and congratulations on your efforts. You have been admitted by CQU, a palace of academy with profound cultural accumulation!

Your academic career will turn a new page from today on. Students who will achieve master degrees should be masters of academic research, and a considerable number of them make a living by research. What we study on are, of course, academics and knowledge creation. "We learn the changes and gain knowledge in universal way to create a philosophy of one's own." The so-called "creating a philosophy of one's own" is what we often call "innovation". Innovation is the soul of academic research, which means that we must expand the fields that our predecessors have not been involved in. It is not always a bed of roses but the one covered with twists and thorns. As it is said by Marx, "There is no smooth avenue in science; only those who climb a steep mountain road can be likely to reach the culmination of glory." I have to say that engaging in scholarship is an activity that requires much hard work and creativity, and it needs a spirit to support it. Students must maintain a spirit of daring to climb to the peak regardless of pains and pangs.

做学问呼唤工匠精神

—— 在重庆大学2016级研究生开学典礼上的讲话

亲爱的同学们：

大家上午好！

伴随着山城初秋的凉爽，重庆大学迎来了4 700名研究生新同学。首先，我代表学校对你们表示热烈的欢迎，也祝贺你们通过自己的努力，如愿进入重大这座具有深厚文化积淀的学术殿堂！

从今天开始，你们的学术生涯将翻开新的一页。作为研究生，顾名思义就是从事研究的学生，其中相当一部分人甚至要"以研究为生"。研究什么呢，当然是研究学术、创造知识，"究天人之际，通古今之变，成一家之言"。所谓"成一家之言"，就是我们常说的"创新"。创新是学术研究的灵魂，意味着要拓展前人未曾涉足的领域，这并非一条康庄大道，往往充满艰辛，布满荆棘，正如马克思所言："在科学上没有平坦的大道，只有不畏劳苦沿着陡峭山路攀登的人，才有希望达到光辉的顶点。"不得不说，做学问是一项十分艰苦的创造性活动，需要有一种精神来支撑，同学们务必保持一股不畏劳苦、

Today, I want to talk to you about the significance of craftsmanship spirit for graduate students in study.

What is the craftsmanship spirit? The long-standing craftsmanship of Chinese civilization is highlighted in skills of ancient Chinese of all walks such as tools-inventing of craftsman Luban, car-making of official Xi Zhong, ox-dissecting of Chef Ding, and core-carving of artist Wang Shuyuan; in the ancient Chinese arts like the brilliant Peking Opera and the marvelous oral stunts; and in the ancient Chinese handicrafts including the fine Four-ram Zun and exquisite pieces made of four famous embroideries. All major inventions or creations in the world are the products of craftsmanship spirit. Edison finally invented the electric lamp after thousands of failures; Madam Curie extracted one tenth of a gram of radium from several tons of asphalt uranium slag; Mendel spent 8 years experimenting with 32 varieties of pea before revealing the Heredity Law; Sima Qian endured humiliation but insisted on writing and took 13 years to conduct his work which become a masterpiece; Li Shizhen tasted hundreds of herbs, visited other well-known doctors and asked for medicine, and after 26 years, he completed the masterpiece *Compendium of Materia Medica*. But today we do not seem to have inherited such a fine tradition well. As in the most noticeable manufacturing country, due to the lack of craftsmanship spirit, products made in China have left a stereotype of "cheapness and low quality". In the academic world, the atmosphere is also becoming more and more impetuous and the phenomenon of pursuing quick success and instant benefits often happens, which demonstrates that the craftsmanship spirit is urgently called by the times.

Craftsmanship spirit, in short, is the pursuit of excellence, the attitude of working to be ever better and the spirit of staying rigorous and hard-working. It coincides with the motto of Chongqing University — "Endurance, Frugality, Diligence, Patriotism". It is the spirit that graduate students need to learn. So how shall we nurture craftsmanship spirit on the academic road?

First, be rigorous.

Rigorousness is the cornerstone of the craftsmanship spirit. Academic study is an honest work which demands researchers to be rigorous and pragmatic because the least bit of difference will hack the truth away. Guo Moruo once said that science calls for conscientious academic research and can't bear any fault at all. With a population of 80 million, Germany boasts more than 2,300 world-famous brands. The reason why Germany has become a manufacturing giant is in the words of Siemens founder, Werner von Siemens, that it depends on the German work attitude

敢于攀登的精气神。我今天想给大家谈谈做学问需要的"工匠精神"，谈谈工匠精神对研究生学习的重要意义。

什么是工匠精神？古之中国技人，如鲁班之百工、奚仲之造车、庖丁之解牛、叔远之雕核；古之中国技艺，如京剧之绝伦、口技之绝妙；古之中国艺器，如四羊方尊之精致、四大名绣之精美，无不彰显着中华文明源远流长的工匠精神。世界上的重大发明或创造无一不是工匠精神的产物。爱迪生经过上千次的实验失败终于发明了电灯；居里夫人从几吨沥青铀矿渣中提炼出十分之一克的镭元素；孟德尔用8年时间试验了32个豌豆品种才揭示了遗传定律；司马迁忍辱偷生、笔耕不辍，历时13年而成"史家之绝唱，无韵之离骚"；李时珍遍尝百草、访医问药，历时26年而成《本草纲目》。反观现在，我们似乎并没有很好地继承这样的优良传统，作为最令人瞩目的制造大国，因为工匠精神的缺失，"中国制造"已给人们留下"廉价低质"的刻板印象。在学术界，风气也日趋浮躁，做学问急功近利、粗制滥造的现象时有发生。由此可见，重拾工匠精神为时代所呼唤。

工匠精神，简单地说，就是精益求精、追求卓越的精神品格，是没有最好、只有更好的工作态度，是严谨踏实、勤奋刻苦的钻研精神。它与重庆大学"耐劳苦、尚俭朴、勤学业、爱国家"的校训可谓不谋而合，研究生做学问需要的就是这种精神。那么，在学术道路上我们要如何培育工匠精神？

第一，要严谨踏实。

严谨踏实是工匠精神的根基。做学问是一项诚实的劳动，必须严谨踏实，不能有丝毫不严不实，如果"差之毫厘"，则可能"谬以千里"。正如郭沫若所说，"科学是老老实实的学问，来不得半点虚假"。8 000万人口的德国，竟然有2 300多个世界名牌。德国之所以成为制造强国，用西门子公司创始人维尔纳·冯·西门子的话说："这靠的

and high degree of emphasis on the details related to technologies and production.

We must maintain the bottom line of academic integrity. In recent years, in order to get degrees, titles, and finishing projects, some people have tampered with experimental data and even forged research results and copied the academic achievements of others, which are totally contrary to the craftsmanship spirit. In last April, a large British medical academic institution withdrew 43 articles, of which 41 were from Chinese authors. "Cultivate the leaves before you grow the flowers, and nourish the roots before the leaves." I hope that you will take a serious and responsible attitude towards each investigation, experiment, datum, and derivation in your studies, to adhere to academic ethics and abide by academic norms, to be reasonable and justified, and to treat the "quality of your paper" as your "personality". Never be expedient, or otherwise, it will be biting off your own head, and doing harm to others and yourself eventually.

Secondly, be diligent and pragmatic.

Hard work is the soul of the craftsmanship spirit. An old saying goes that "Efficiency comes from diligence, idleness from neglect; accomplishment is obtained from thoughts but failure from blindly following the trend." It is difficult to engage in scholarship unless you are diligent and pragmatic. Success is the result of diligence without no exception. American writer Malcolm Gladwell once said that "The reason why talented people are remarkable is not their superior talent, but sustained efforts. Ten thousand hours of temper is necessary for the mediocre to become extraordinary."

To be diligent and pragmatic, you must persist in the spirit of hard work. The core of the 12-character motto of Chongqing University is "Diligence". To be diligent, first of all, to be dedicated. Churchill once said that "It is no use doing what you like; you have got to like what you are doing." When you choose your major, I hope that you could choose what you love and love what you have chosen and love it as if it is your model. There is an old saying that "For those people who are not successful in their work or study, they cannot blame on their talent or other people but the lack of concentration."[1] Professor Jiang Xingliang in the School of Electrical Engineering of our university mainly studies the external insulation and ice prevention and disaster reduction of the power grid under extremely harsh environments, spending almost one-third of each year in extremely harsh places with coldness, high humidity and hypoxia. Though calluses spread all his hands just like hands of migrant workers,

---

1   From Song Lian in the Ming Dynasty. It means that if you are not proficient in academics or not perfect at morals, it is not because you are lack of talents, but because your mind is not focused.

是德国人的工作态度，以及对每个生产技术细节的重视。"

要做到严谨踏实，必须守住学术诚信的底线。近年来，一些人为学位、为职称、为项目在研究中篡改实验数据，伪造研究结果，抄袭他人学术成果。这些都与工匠精神背道而驰。去年4月，英国某大型医学学术机构撤刊了43篇文章，其中41篇论文来自中国作者。"养花先养叶，养叶先养根"，我希望同学们在学习研究中对每一项调研、每一次试验、每一个数据、每一步推导，都要以认真负责的态度来对待；要坚持学术道德，恪守学术规范，言从理出，论由据起，把"文格"看如"人格"，绝不苟且，绝不权宜，否则终将害人误己。

第二，要勤奋务实。

勤奋务实是工匠精神的灵魂。古人云："业精于勤，荒于嬉；行成于思，毁于随。"做学问是一件辛苦的事，必须勤奋务实，不能有丝毫懒惰懈怠。但凡任何所谓的成功，无一不是勤奋努力的结果。美国作家马尔科姆·格拉德威尔说："人们眼中的天才之所以卓越非凡，并非天资超人一等，而是付出了持续不断的努力。一万小时的锤炼是任何人从平凡变成超凡的必要条件。"

要做到勤奋务实，必须坚持刻苦钻研的精神。重庆大学12字校训，核心就是要"勤学业"。要"勤业首先需要"敬业"。丘吉尔曾说，不能爱哪行才干哪行，要干哪行爱哪行。我希望同学们对待你们的专业，要选你所爱，爱你所选，将自己的专业当成心目中的"男神""女神"一样去爱慕、去追求。古人云，"其业有不精，德有不成者，非天质之卑，则心不若余之专耳，岂他人之过哉"[1]。我校电气工程学院蒋兴良教授主要研究极端恶劣环境下电网外绝缘、覆冰与防冰减灾，一年差不多三分之一的时间都在寒冷、高湿和缺氧等极端恶劣

---

[1] 出自明代宋濂《送东阳马生序》。意思是学业不精通、德行不具备，不是因为天赋不够，而是思想不专注，这不是别人的过失。

he finally successfully completed more than 50 major projects such as West-East Power Transmission, Three Gorges Project, Qinghai-Tibet Railway UHV, etc., and successively won the first prize of the National Science and Technology Progress Award, and the second prize twice. His story told us that we should specialize in our profession, studying extensively and comprehensively. Only by focusing on your own profession with persistence and diligence can you achieve success.

Thirdly, be innovative and pragmatic.

Innovation and realism are at the core of the craftsmanship spirit. Literally, "craftsman" and "innovation" don not seem to have much connection. "Craftsman" focuses on the monotonous work at hand day after day while "innovation" emphasizes the creation and update of theories and research. However, real innovation is not water without any source or a tree without roots. A little bit of thinking and continuous sublimation along with mechanical repetition makes the great innovation. The spirit of craftsmanship is not a lockstep but a process of continuous creation based on tradition and a coexistence of inheritance and innovation. It can be seen that the spirit of craftsmanship is the foundation of innovation while innovation is the sublimation of the spirit of craftsmanship; the spirit of craftsmanship promotes the development of innovation while the spirit of innovation leads the spirit of craftsmanship. The spirit of craftsmanship contains a power of innovation. Otherwise, why is it "ingenuity"? Study is a process of constant repetition, continuous innovation, and seeking new knowledge. Craftsmanship is a quality that innovative talents must possess.

To be innovative and realistic, you must persist in brave discovery and exploration, since innovation means to question and make a breakthrough on old theories, ideas, conclusions, and even challenge authorities. Scientific research is the exploration and creation of the future. It must inherit the achievements of its predecessors and at the same time overcome blind obedience. I hope that students could think and explore more based on your research direction to find an innovative method suitable for yourselves and the open sesame to scientific truth. Set out to discover, to invent, to create, and to make some difference. Go to appreciate and enjoy the joy of seeking truth and overcome difficulties to create a new path and achieve success.

Fourthly, never seek quick success and instant benefits.

Never seek quick success and instant benefits, which is the prerequisite for the craftsmanship spirit. Study is a painful cultivation journey. We must be indifferent to fame and fortune, and have a calm mindset. We cannot seek quick success and instant benefits or chase fame and fortune. You may be perfunctory because of the

的地方，"扛锄头挖土石，磨起老茧像民工"，最终圆满完成了西电东送、三峡工程、青藏铁路特高压等重大项目 50 余项，先后获国家科技进步奖一等奖 1 次、二等奖 2 次。这告诉我们，术业有专攻。广学而博，专一而精；只有专注于自己的专业，踏实执着，加倍勤奋，方能有所成就。

第三，要创新求实。

创新求实是工匠精神的核心。就字面而言，"工匠"与"创新"似乎没有太多联系。"工匠"们日复一日专注于自己手头单调的工作，而"创新"强调的是创造和出新。但是，真正的创新并非无源之水、无本之木，单调、机械重复中的一点点思考不断升华就成就了伟大的创新。工匠精神不是因循守旧，它是在传统基础上不断创造的过程，是一种传承与创新的并存。由此可见，工匠精神是创新的基础，创新是工匠精神的升华；工匠精神推动着创新的发展，创新精神又引领着工匠精神。工匠精神蕴含着一种创新的力量，不然，何来"匠心独具"？做学问是一个不断反复、不断创新、探求新知的过程，工匠精神是创新性人才必须具备的品质。

要做到创新求实，必须坚持大胆发现，勇于探索。这是因为，创新意味着要对旧理论、旧观念、旧结论的怀疑和突破，甚至要对权威进行挑战。科学研究是对未来的探索和创造，既要继承前人的成果，又要克服盲从并开拓创新。我希望同学们要结合自己的研究方向，多思考、多探索，找到适合自己的创新方法，叩开科学真理的大门，有所发现、有所发明、有所创造、有所作为，并在研究中体会和享受那种探求真理、克服困难、独辟蹊径、取得成功的愉悦。

第四，要淡泊平实。

淡泊平实是工匠精神的前提。做学问就是一场"精神苦旅"的修行，必须淡泊名利、心态平实，不能心气浮躁、追逐名利。当你在地

disagreeable environment when you perform environmental tests in a mine 100 meters below the ground, when you collect data at an overhead transmission line workstation in a high-altitude area, or when you conduct logistics control monitoring at a railway freight station. Treating academic research with a passive attitude will drive you farther from the spirit of craftsmanship. Einstein noted that the value of a person hinges on what contribution he has made. Only by setting up the correct values and asking only the truth regardless of the interests can we nourish real craftsmanship spirit.

Being plain and quiet in mind with few desires, we must be able to withstand loneliness and temptations. Nowadays, the outside world and even universities are full of temptation. But impetuousness is the "natural enemy" of study. We must buckle down and calm down, keep a quiet mind and maintain the inner peace. We can't regard study as a tool to get our "bread", nor a platform for getting rich. Everything in university should be "only for study". At the same time, study needs a fine workmanship, which means that you may not get the result quickly. We need to have the ethics and perseverance that even if we would not have one visitor for ten years, we should not write one improper word in paper; and also have the patience and determination of maintaining still and strong, no matter how harsh the outside environment is. Only in this way can we conduct real academic research.

Dear students, our school is committed to making a first-class comprehensive research-oriented university in southwestern China, with unique characteristics and international fame and advancing all-front reforms and the construction of "first-class university with first-class disciplines". Postgraduates are a creative group full of vigor and vitality, who serve as a vital force for academic research in universities as well as an important embodiment of the quality and scholarship of a university. The university will further deepen the reform of graduate education and make every effort to provide each student with a suitable development platform. As the president and a tutor for graduate students, I am eagerly looking forward that you could uphold the craftsmanship spirit in the academic field at Chongqing University and train yourselves as "skillful craftsmen" for scientific research. You should work hard and dare to innovate and try your best to climb the academic peak. You are supposed to contribute your talents to building a world-class university, and to reserve power for the realization of the Chinese Dream of the great rejuvenation of the Chinese nation.

Finally, I wish you all a good time at Chongqing University!

Thank you all!

面以下一百米的矿井进行环境测试时，当你在高海拔地区架空输电线路工作站采集数据时，当你在铁路货运站进行物流调控监测时，你也许会因为环境艰苦而敷衍了事，用"做一天和尚撞一天钟"的心态对待学问、对待学习，这样你将离工匠精神愈来愈远。爱因斯坦说，一个人的价值，应该看他贡献什么。只有树立起正确的价值观，"只问是非，不计利害"，我们才可能具备真正的工匠精神。

要做到淡泊平实，必须耐得住寂寞，经得住诱惑。今天这个时代，"外面的世界很精彩"，学校也并非一方净土，我们每天都经受着各种诱惑。但浮躁是做学问的"天敌"，我们必须要沉下心来，保持清静的心态，淡定从容、独守宁静。我们不能把学习仅仅当作找"饭碗"的工具，也不能把学习当作致富为官的平台，一切都应只"为求学而来"。同时，做学问是一件"慢活"，难以速成，我们要有"板凳要坐十年冷，文章不写半句空"的操守和毅力，要有"千磨万击还坚劲，任尔东西南北风"的耐心和定力。只有这样，才能做出真学问。

同学们，学校已明确了"树西南风声、创一流大学"的办学目标，正全面深化综合改革，推进"一流大学一流学科"建设。研究生是充满朝气和活力、富有创新精神的群体，是大学学术科研的生力军，也是办学质量、学术水平的重要体现。学校将进一步深化研究生教育改革，尽力给每位同学提供适宜的发展平台。作为校长和一名研究生导师，我热切期盼你们在重大这片学术热土上秉持工匠精神，把自己锻炼成科学研究的"能工巧匠"，潜心耕耘，敢于创新，勇攀学术高峰，为把重庆大学建设成为世界一流大学奉献才智，为实现中华民族伟大复兴的中国梦储备力量。

最后，祝愿大家在重庆大学度过美好时光！

谢谢大家！

Blossom in Plainness, Dream in Common

—Speech at the 2015 Graduation Ceremony of Chongqing University

Dear students,

As time flies, another summer is coming as expected. There are groups of students in academic costumes posing for pictures on campus with relaxation or seriousness on their face. The joy of graduation and the sentimentality of parting are intertwined at this moment. Sometimes I came across some students taking photos in front of office buildings and was invited to join them. Comparing the shyness and timidity you had a few years ago with the cultured temperament and the blooming faces when you are wearing now, I feel happy for you; even if I am busy, I will stop and gladly accept your invitations. I am honored to witness your growth.

Of course, today's graduation ceremony is the best witness of your growth in university, especially when today's hot weather sets off the warm atmosphere on the scene. On this solemn occasion, on behalf of the school, I sincerely congratulate you on your completion of your studies! I am also willing to express the most sincere thanks with you to the teachers, classmates, friends and families who have helped you along the way!

Time goes by so fast that we cannot seize it even for a second. The day we met was as if yesterday, but now parting is approaching. After years of studying and living here, I believe that you have all walked into the arms of Chongqing University, and Chongqing University has already lived in your heart. Your friendship with

平凡的世界会有人懂你

—— 在重庆大学 2015 届学生毕业典礼上的讲话

亲爱的同学们：

　　时光流转，又一个夏天如约而至，校园里随处可见三五成群穿着学位服合影留念的身影，或嬉笑，或严肃，毕业的喜悦和离别的感伤都交织定格在这一瞬间。有时在办公楼前会"偶遇"照相的同学，落落大方地邀请我一起合影。品味同学们身着学位服的文雅气质，看着年轻脸庞绽放出的奕奕神采，对比几年前入学时的羞涩腼腆、怯手怯脚，我由衷地为你们感到高兴；即使再忙我都会停下脚步欣然应允，能在镜头前站在你们身旁见证你们的成长我非常荣幸。

　　当然，今天的毕业典礼才是你们大学成长最好的见证，尤其是今天的高温天气，烘托着现场热烈的气氛。在这庄严的时刻，我代表学校衷心祝贺你们圆满地完成了学业！我也很愿意和你们一道，向帮助你们一路走来的老师、同学、朋友以及家人表达最诚挚的谢意！

your fellow students and teachers in CQU will become your lifetime attachment and memory. I know that you have complained about the hot water, the food, the Internet, and the limited seats in study rooms... Although we already have the enviable air conditioners and libraries called "amenities only in other universities" by students of other universities, we must make Chongqing University better. Anyway, no matter how happy or hard the past on the campus was, it will become a permanent treasure of your life.

Just now, the school commended the outstanding graduates, among whom there are super scholars who have come out in front, research stars who have buckled down to academics, pioneering entrepreneurs who have braved to start up their business, and young volunteers who are enthusiastic about public welfare. They have won your applause. However, I would like to give my praise to many students who are working diligently and silently but failing to receive any compliment. Maybe your grades are not high enough, but you are humorous and optimistic, because of which your classmates all like you. Maybe you have not published a high-level scientific research paper, but after reading such classics you have already possessed a quick thinking and outstanding eloquence. Maybe you don't have the qualifications to start a business and you don't have your own office, but you have a wide range of interests and innovations to organize the student community in perfect order. Maybe you are not engaged in public welfare, but you are caring and easy-going and are the "timely rain" for classmates. All the scenes seem to be bland but actually conducting the splendid scroll of Chongqing University. You are all the best in this way, and I applaud you.

In fact, it is same to our life. Subjected to the environment, reality and our own conditions, we cannot all become people of accomplishment in the conventional sense. Most of us are just ordinary members of society. You have struggled all the way from elementary school, middle school to university, and have experienced fierce competitions. It seems that only the recognized talents are the winners and the vast majority the losers. Such a judgment is a bit narrow. I hope that you can understand the meaning of "success" more profoundly. During the "World Reading Day" this year, Guangming Online invited me to recommend a book, and I picked *World of Plainness* by Lu Yao. There is a sentence in this book: "Everyone's life is also a world, and even the most ordinary one has to fight for the existence of his world." Yes, the comparison is meaningless since everyone has their own world. In my opinion,

"时间太瘦，指缝太宽"[1]，日子总是不经意地从我们指缝间悄然溜走。相识犹如昨日，可离别就在眼前。经过这几年的学习生活，相信你们都"走进"了重大的怀里，重大也"住进"了你们的心间，你们在重大所结下的同窗情、师生谊都将成为你们今生挥别不了的眷恋。我知道，你们对学校也曾有所抱怨，吐槽热水不够热、饭菜不够香、网速有点慢、自习室的座位要靠"抢"……，你们的抱怨让我知道，尽管我们已经拥有了让外校学生羡慕的"别人家的空调"和"别人家的图书馆"[2]，但我们还必须让重大变得更好。不管怎样，无论苦乐，那些历历在目的校园往事都将成为你们一生永久的珍藏。

刚才，学校对优秀的毕业生进行了表彰，他们中有一路领先的学神学霸，有潜心学术的科研新星，有勇于开拓的创业达人，也有热心公益的青年志愿者，他们赢得了全场的掌声。但我在这里还要为台下众多积极努力、默默奋斗却未能获得表彰的同学们用力点赞。也许你的成绩不够拔尖，但是你风趣幽默、乐观向上，同学们都喜欢你的正能量；也许你没有发表高水平的科研论文，但是你熟读经典、才思敏捷，一不小心就能出口成章；也许你不具备创业的条件，没有创办自己的工作室，但是你兴趣广泛、推陈出新，把一个学生社团做得有模有样；也许你没有从事公益，但是你富有爱心、善解人意，是同学们心目中的"及时雨"；……这些看似平淡无奇，但是如果没有你们这一道道亮丽的风景，就成就不了重庆大学一幅幅精彩的画卷。从这一点来讲，你们都是最优秀的，我要为你们鼓掌！

其实，我们的人生也是如此，受环境、现实和自身条件的约束，我们不可能人人都成为常规意义的"成功者"，我们绝大部分人都只

1　源自安意如的作品《当时只道是寻常》，形容时间过得太快，总在你不经意间悄悄流逝。

2　网络流行语言，表达一种羡慕之情。

you're successful as long as you live and study making full use of your energy and abtainable resources. It is precisely because of such different successes that constitute the rich lives and the colorful world. Perhaps we are all "farsighted", always living in looking up at others, and ignoring the happiness around us. I want to tell you that we are all ordinary people, because we are all from the "ordinary world", but we can all succeed, as long as we strive to do our best in our worlds, do every ordinary thing around us well.

As a graduate of Chongqing University, it is also true that you may not all become so-called "elites" in society, but I believe that even if you are ordinary members of society, you are also backbones for propelling the movement of society. Today, you are seeds scattered throughout society, taking your roots and thriving in your ordinary worlds; as Lu Yao said, "I want to live a realistic life. However, sometimes, I would like to jump out from the real life and peep on the platform named dream", in realizing self-value and fulfilling family and social responsibilities, gathering the power of countless "ordinary people" thereby promoting social development, national rejuvenation and the prosperity of a country, as CQUers, we should shoulder the social responsibility of "rejuvenating the nation and vowing to be the striker". In the future, whether you are going to be a designer, a host, a judge, or a soldier ..., your hard work is the "pushing hands" of this era! Although you are in a world of plainness, there must be someone understanding you!

We long for achievement but we must accept plainness which is more normal in life. In the torrent of progress of the times, it is not easy to go up, and harder to let it go. In this era of rapid information development, the entrepreneurial story of Ma Huateng[1], the full passion of Steve Jobs that "we are here to put a dent in the universe" and some so-called "successful studies" that surround us through the Internet showed us the mirages of "success" which seem so close and easy to touch. But in this world, not all "reasonable" and "beautiful" things can exist or be realized as you wish. The whole society will be proud of you for your great achievements; your families, friends and the society will as well applaud you if you lead a happy life though without accomplishments, staying true and striving to be better, rather than looking up in the glory of others. The modern poet Bian Zhilin once said, " You stand on the bridge viewing the sight; You're beheld by the viewer from height." Much of

---

1   Also known as Pony Ma, is the founder, chairman and CEO of Tencent, one of the most valuable companies in Asia.

是社会中平凡的一员。你们从小学、中学到大学一路拼搏而上，经历着激烈的竞争，好像只有这样才是最优秀、才会被社会认可、才是成功者，而绝大多数人都是失败者。这样的评判有些狭隘，我希望把"成功"的内涵理解得更加深刻。今年"世界读书日"期间，"光明网"请我推荐书目，我推荐了路遥的《平凡的世界》。书中有这样一句话："每个人的生活同样也是一个世界。即使最平凡的人，也得要为他那个世界的存在而战斗。"是的，一个人有一个人的世界，不同世界的比较毫无意义。我认为，只要你在自己的世界里，对人生充满希望，竭尽所能，发挥出自己的能量，那就是成功。正因为有了这样不同意义的成功，才构成了我们生活的丰富多彩和世界的五彩斑斓。或许，我们都是"远视眼"，总是活在对别人的仰视里，而忽略了身边的幸福。我想给大家说，我们都是平凡人，因为我们都来自"平凡的世界"；但我们都可以成功，只要我们在自己的世界里尽力去奋斗，把身边每一件平凡的事做好，你就是成功的人！

作为重大的毕业生，也是如此，我们不可能人人都成为社会所谓的"精英"，但我相信，即便我们作为社会平凡的一员也将是推动社会进步的中坚力量。我会看到你们，像散播于社会各处的种子，在自己的平凡世界里，生根发芽，茁壮成长；就像路遥说的那样，"既要脚踏实地于现实生活，又要不时跳出现实到理想的高台上张望一眼"，在实现自我价值和履行家庭与社会责任的过程中，影响和聚集起身边无数"平凡人"的力量，从而推动社会的发展、民族的复兴和国家的富强，在平凡中承载起我们重大人"复兴民族兮，誓作前锋"的社会担当。将来，不管你是手拿图纸，还是手捧话筒；是手持法槌，还是手握钢枪……，你勤劳的双手就是这个时代前进的"推手"！尽管你身处平凡的世界，但在平凡的世界里一定会有人懂你！

平凡是生活的常态，我们渴望有所"成就"，但一定要接受平凡。

同学们，从母校起程的人生列车已经停靠在你的身旁，悠扬的汽笛正在离别的喧嚣中回荡。"笔下画不完的圆，心间填不满的缘"[1]，都是母校对你们永久的期盼和挂念！挥别昨天的你，怀着离别的情，带着勇敢的心，在广阔的天地里，奔跑吧，同学们[2]！

谢谢大家！

1 电影《何以笙箫默》主题插曲中的歌词，表达对母校依依不舍的情感。
2 借用浙江卫视正热播的综艺节目《奔跑吧兄弟》，鼓励同学们勇敢地走向社会。

CQU Spirit Guides You

—Speech at the Opening Ceremony of 2015 Undergraduates of Chongqing University

Dear students,

With the same pursuit and perseverance, 6,325 students meet today in Chongqing University. As the president, I would like to sincerely congratulate you on your achievements made in the college entrance examination, and on behalf of all the teachers and students warmly welcome you to Chongqing University!

A lifelong bond will be created between you and CQU from today on. Here at the campus, you will enjoy beautiful scenery all year round, including cherry blossoms in spring, lotus flowers in summer, golden ginkgoes in autumn and plum blossoms in winter. There in CQU is combination of tradition and modernity, joint improvement of science, technology and humanities, and mutual learning of teachers and students, and you will spend the best time of your life in CQU!

CQU toady is what our predecessors looked forward to. The military parade for the 70th anniversary of the victory of the Chinese People's War of Resistance Against Japanese Aggression and the Global War Against Fascism eight days ago made us proud of our motherland and realize that our personal destinies depend on the strength of our motherland. Founded in in 1929, a year of turbulence when Chongqing municipality was established, CQU witnessed Japan's invasion into China less than two years later. Since then, the fate of CQU has been ever closely linked to that of the nation. During the War of Resistance Against Japanese

让重大精神指引你前进的方向

—— 在重庆大学 2015 级本科生开学典礼上的讲话

亲爱的同学们：

怀着相同的追求与梦想，凭着同样的坚毅与执着，6 325 名优秀学子今天相逢嘉陵江畔，齐聚歌乐山下，携手走进彼此共同向往的重庆大学。此刻，作为校长，我要衷心祝贺你们在刚刚过去的高考中蟾宫折桂，也代表重大全体师生热情欢迎你们成为光荣的"重大人"！

从今天起，你们就和重大结下了终身的"学缘"，可谓"学在于斯，缘定于此"。在这里，春有樱花烂漫、夏有荷叶连连、秋有银杏金黄、冬有蜡梅飘香，无论是晨曦山色，还是夕阳湖光，都令人神怡心旷；在这里，传统与现代共融、科技与人文并举、大师与学子相长，涵养书香、学术日新的重大将陪伴你们度过人生最美好的时光！

这美妙的光景曾是多少重大先辈的期盼！八天前"抗战胜利日"阅兵让我们不禁为祖国的强大而感到自豪，也深切感受到强大祖国与个人命运是如此息息相关。1929 年，重庆大学诞生于风雨飘摇的年代，与重庆建市同年。建校后不到两年，日本帝国主义就发动了侵华

Aggression, the national government relocated the capital in Chongqing, making it one of the four major command of the Global War Against Fascism centers along with Washington, London, and Moscow. Against the Japanese bombing for five and a half years, the army and civilians in Chongqing made great sacrifices and contributions to the Global War Against Fascism with their indomitable spirit. As the top university in this heroic city, CQU led her teachers and students to dedicate themselves to teaching, learning and scientific research, and participate in the resistance movement fighting against the Japanese aggression at the same time. They wrote a heroic historical chapter with their flesh and blood. Today, I'm going to tell you CQUers' heroic deeds in the War of Resistance .

Let's start with Liu Xiang, the founder of Chongqing University, Commander of the Sichuan Army and Chairman of Sichuan province during the period of the Republic of China. As the first president of CQU between 1929 and 1935, Mr. Liu made indelible contributions to the university's development. After the Lugou Bridge Incident in 1937, Mr. Liu made a nearly-two-hour inspiring speech at the Defense Conference of the national government, giving his proposition to "mobilize the whole country and fight to the death with Japan", clearly opposing the policy of "first pacifying the interior before resisting foreign aggression", and offering to fight against Japan and defend the country. Representatives of the Communist Party of China including Zhou Enlai, Zhu De and Ye Jianying visited Liu Xiang and praised his determination. People around all persuaded him from fighting the war considering his illness, but he said, "I used to fight the civil war for years, which was a bit dishonored. I will never allow myself to hide in the rear in face of the urgent need of serving the country." Liu Xiang led his troop to join in the War of Resistance Against Japanese Aggression, but unfortunately, he fell ill on the front line and died in Hankou in 1938. Before his death, he left a will, "Until the end of the war will we never give up", which greatly boosted the morale of the Sichuan Army. Every day when the flag was raised, officers and soldiers recited his will in unison to show their determination. This is our honorable president Liu Xiang.

The second story is about Feng Jian, the founder of China's radio research, the first Chinese to carry on a scientific expedition to the Arctic, and professor of electrical engineering at Chongqing University. Professor Feng graduated from Cornell University in 1924 with a master's degree. In 1938, he was employed as professor and head of the Electrical Engineering Department. From 1941 to 1949,

战争，从此，重庆大学就与国家和民族的命运紧紧相连。抗战时期，国民政府内迁重庆，重庆同华盛顿、伦敦、莫斯科一道被列为世界反法西斯四大指挥中心。重庆军民面对日寇飞机持续五年半的疯狂轰炸，以坚韧不拔的精神为世界反法西斯战争做出了巨大牺牲和重大贡献。作为这座英雄城市的最高学府，重庆大学奋发图强，广大师生同仇敌忾，一边坚持教学科研，一边积极投入抗日救亡运动和直接对敌作战，用热血和生命谱写了可歌可泣的英雄壮歌。今天，我就给大家讲讲"重大人"的抗战故事。

我们先从重庆大学的创始人刘湘说起。刘湘是民国时期川军统帅、四川省主席，作为重庆大学主要创始人，于1929年至1935年出任第一任校长，为重庆大学的起步做出了不可磨灭的贡献。1937年"卢沟桥事变"后，刘湘在国民政府国防会议上极力主张"全国总动员，与日本拼死一决"，慷慨陈词近两小时，明确反对"攘外必先安内"的政策，主动请缨出川对日作战。会后，出席会议的中共代表周恩来、朱德、叶剑英等亲临刘湘寓所访问，赞誉他积极抗战的决心。身边人劝多病的刘湘不必亲征，留在四川。刘湘说："过去打了多年内战，脸面上不甚光彩，今天为国效命，如何可以在后方苟安！"之后，刘湘亲率部队出川抗战，但在抗战前线突发疾病，1938年在汉口去世，逝前留有遗嘱："抗战到底，始终不渝，即敌军一日不退出国境，川军则一日誓不还乡！"刘湘的遗嘱极大地鼓舞了前线川军的士气，每天升旗时，官兵必同声诵读，以示抗战到底的决心。这就是值得我们尊敬的刘湘校长！

第二个故事讲的是我国无线电研究的创始人、中国赴北极科考第一人、重庆大学电机系教授冯简先生。冯简教授1924年在美国康奈尔大学硕士毕业，1938年受聘我校电机系，担任教授和系主任，1941年至1949年担任我校工学院院长。抗战初期，冯简教授作为资深专

he served the dean of the Engineering College of CQU. In the early days of the War of Resistance , Professor Feng presided over the construction of the China Radio International, China's first 35-kilowatt short-wave radio station. After the outbreak of the Attack on Pearl Harbor in 1941, most of the radio stations of the Allies in the Far East against fascism fell into Japanese hands. The China Radio International became the only available hub for the Allies in the Far East. Foreign journalists in Chongqing at that time used the station to broadcast and distribute news reports, and the crimes of militarism and the unyielding voice of China were sent from here to the world. The Japanese aggressors were so frustrated that they were carefully deployed to bombard this station. However, the radio station escaped many disasters and was honed under the meticulous maintenance of Professor Feng and the students. The helpless enemy felt the "never-ending" sound of the radio like the annoying frog, nicknamed the station "Frog of Chongqing". In August 1945, the news of "Japan's unconditional surrender" was spread from the "Frog of Chongqing" throughout China.

During the War of Resistance, CQU was repeatedly bombed by the Japanese army, and the bombing caused disastrous casualties and property damage. Among them, spectacular Xingzi Zhai Building less than 10 years old was razed to the ground, the two buildings of the Engineering College fortunately survived from the bombing and was later restored and retained to become today's Teaching Building No. 2. At that time, teachers and students built a large bombing monument with broken bricks and stones that still stands next to the Teaching Building No. 2. The war is a purgatory and melting pot; the crueler the enemy is, the stronger we will be. CQU survived the disaster and grew even stronger, and had gone through difficulties and hardships together with the nation. Teachers and students actively participated in the movement for resistance against Japanese aggression and national salvation, and made speeches to people at all levels in the society to express the determination to fight against the Japanese invaders to the end. Comrade Zhou Enlai was invited to give a speech, which inspired teachers and students to strengthen their belief in the victory of the war and set off a new high tide of resistance against Japanese aggression to save the country. He Qichen, a 40-Grade student majoring electromechanics, gave up his study and went to the United States where he was trained to be a member of the American Volunteer Group, serving as the captain of the B-25 Bomber and won many battles. CQU also actively played the role in education on the home

家在重庆主持修建了我国第一座 35 千瓦短波电台，即"中国国际广播电台"。1941 年"珍珠港事件"爆发后，远东反法西斯各盟国电台尽落入日本之手，该电台成为盟军在远东唯一可用的联络枢纽。当时在重庆的国外记者都利用这个电台转播和发稿，军国主义的罪行和中国不屈的声音都是从这里源源不断地向全球发出的。日寇深感头痛，周密部署对其重点轰炸，但该电台躲过重重劫难，在冯简教授和学生们的精心维护下雄鸣不止，使其成为一座坚不可摧的精神丰碑。无可奈何的敌人感觉"无休止"的电台声音就像令人烦躁的蛙声，谑称此电台为"重庆之蛙"。1945 年 8 月"日本无条件投降"的消息就是从"重庆之蛙"传遍中华大地的。

抗战期间，重庆大学遭到日军多次轰炸，师生伤亡和财产损失十分惨重。其中，建成不到十年蔚为壮观的行字斋和工学院两栋大楼正中炮弹，行字斋被夷为平地，所幸工学院大楼经修复后保留了下来，也就是现在 A 校区的"二教"。当时，师生们在废墟中利用破碎的砖石搭建起一座大轰炸纪念碑，纪念碑至今依然矗立在"二教"旁。战争是炼狱，亦是熔炉；敌人愈残暴，我们就愈坚强。刚刚诞生且还处于羸弱中的重庆大学历经这场劫难，不但没有被摧毁，反而在这场波澜壮阔的战斗中，由一个"懵懂少年"迅速成长为一位成熟的"有志青年"，以坚强的意志始终与国家和民族同呼吸、共患难。师生们积极参加抗日救亡运动，深入社会各阶层发表演说，表达和号召与日本侵略者奋战到底的决心；邀请周恩来同志到学校来作形势演讲，师生们深受鼓舞，更加坚定了抗战必胜的信念，掀起了抗日救国的新高潮；40 级机电专业学生何其忱投笔从戎，赴美受训后成为"飞虎队"的一员，任 B-25 型轰炸机机长，屡建战功。重大还积极发挥教育大后方的作用，以宽广的胸怀毅然向内迁至重庆的中央大学伸出了慷慨的双手，提供土地、搭建校舍支持其办学；广泛吸纳各方优秀人

front providing land for building a campus to support the Central University that was just relocated in Chongqing. CQU absorbed talents from all over the country to teach and do research in the university. CQU took the initiative to play the role of the cultural home front, advocating the establishment of the Shapingba-Ciqikou Cultural Area to save the country through education and science, and inherited and developed the spirit of the May Fourth Movement. CQU also gave full play to the role of the academic home front that teachers and students excavated the bomb shelter for building the underground laboratory where they insisted in teaching and doing scientific research. Professors brought their professional skills into play to serve the needs of wartime society. Professor Li Lunjie of the Department of Architecture specially carried out a study on air defense buildings and wartime city planning for air defense, providing suggestions and guidance for Chongqing's air defense construction. After the victory of the War of Resistance Against Japanese Aggression, he presided over the design of the Monument to the People's Liberation in Chongqing.

This duel between life and death, peace and war, light and darkness, civilization and barbarism, forged Chongqing University's spirit that has been passed down from generation to generation, that is, the patriotic spirit of rejuvenating China, the scientific spirit of pursuing truth, hard-working spirit and the innovative spirit of the times. It comes from the unpretentious simplicity of the land of Bayu, and has the same origin with the indomitable spirit of Chongqing people, illuminating the path of great people's progress and coming into being our school motto: Endurance, Frugality, Diligence, Patriotism. It is a torch in the dark, lighting the way of our progress. Under the guidance of this spirit, the university has always stood in the fore front of the reform of higher education, grasping every opportunity to develop, sharing the same fate with the country, advancing with the times. CQU thus has developed into a university with an important strategic position in the national pattern of higher education. Students have been determined to serve the country, and grew into elites as the backbone for national independence and people's liberation, making great contributions to the prosperity of the motherland and human progress!

History is rolling forward. Today, this spiritual torch is passed to you and will continue to lead you to pursue excellence and create history in your own time. Each generation has their own opportunities and interpretations of the CQU spirit. I

才到校任教，大师云集，名家荟萃，构筑了当时中国教育事业的一块高地。主动发挥文化大后方的作用，倡导成立"沙磁文化区"，带头掀起了教育救国、科学救国的热潮，使"五四"新文化运动的精神在这里得到传承与发展。充分发挥学术大后方的作用，师生亲手开挖防空洞，建地下实验室，"顶着轰炸"坚持教学科研；教授们发挥专业特长，服务战时社会需要，建筑系黎抡杰教授就防御空袭专门开展了"防空建筑及战时城市规划"的研究，为重庆防空建设提供建议和指导，抗战胜利后由他主持设计了"抗战胜利纪功碑"，即现在的重庆"解放碑"。

这场生存与死亡、和平与战争、光明与黑暗、文明与野蛮的决斗，锤炼出我们薪火相传的"重大精神"，那就是振兴中华、匹夫有责的爱国精神，崇尚学术、追求真理的科学精神，勤俭朴实、吃苦耐劳的奋斗精神，锐意进取、勇于创新的时代精神。她根植于巴渝大地朴实无华的淳朴民风，与山城儿女顽强不屈的精神同根同源，凝结成我们"耐劳苦、尚俭朴、勤学业、爱国家"的校训。她犹如黑暗中的火炬，照亮重大人进取的道路。在重大精神的指引下，学校始终与国家同风雨、共命运，与时代同前进、共发展，始终以敢为人先的勇气，站在高等教育改革的前列，赢得了学校发展中的每一次重大机遇，使学校发展成为国家高等教育格局中具有重要战略地位的一所大学；广大学生以拳拳报国之志，刻苦用功，勤奋努力，成长为一批批行业精英和国家栋梁，为民族独立、人民解放、祖国繁荣和人类进步做出重大贡献！

历史的车轮滚滚向前，今天，这把精神的火炬传递到了你们的手中，并将继续引领你们在自己所处的时代追求卓越、创造历史。一代人有一代人的际遇和机缘，一代人有一代人对重大精神的诠释，你们作为重大的"新人"，我想给你们几点建议。

would like to give you freshmen some suggestions for studying and living in CQU.

Firstly, harbor patriotic sentiments and have a sense of responsibility.

Sentiments boil down to the nationalism that everyone should be responsible for the prosperity of the country, transferring one's love for individual home to one's homeland. A family is a smallest country, and a country is tens of thousands of families. The fate of individuals is closely linked to that of the country. Being lucky to be born and grow up in a great era, you are ever-closer to achieving the goal of national rejuvenation. Therefore, China today calls for responsible young people instead of spectators. You should care more about the nation and the world. Just as our school song says that "To be in the vanguard of nation rejuvenation, young people should go forward bravely", you should write magnificent youth with patriotic feelings of the country, and bear the mission of endeavours, pioneers and devotees.

Secondly, concern about stars above and care for down-to-earth actions.

Stars above refer to great ambitions and ideals. An ancient saying goes that "You will achieve nothing if you don't have a dream to pursue." Therefore, people first must set great ambitions, and only by combining their personal goals with the dream of the country and the nation will there be a fertile land for dreams. Notice both stars above and down-to-earth actions. Otherwise, dreams will be like water without sources or trees without roots. Achieving your ideals needs perseverance without idling away hours. In class and extra activities, you get to know rules of studying and principles of behaving and the way to live in harmony and adapt to the ever-changing world. It is necessary for you to pay attention to inner cultivation, covering cultivating sound personalities, enhancing civic awareness, and adhering to the principles of life and moral standards, all of which are "the first button of life to be fastened".

Thirdly, admire the outer world and appreciate the inner peace.

In an era of highly developed information that has removed the barrier between universities and the society, the quietness of the campus would be easily broken by the noisy society. In the course of social development, it is impractical and unnecessary to avoid the real society. We should adapt to its changes with an open attitude, enjoy the convenience that technology brings to life, and use the quick ways to understand the world. We should realize that the intuitive thinking caused by the fragmentation of the cognitive world is becoming popular, and the mediocrity of

第一，胸中有情怀，肩上有担当。

"情怀"就是"天下兴亡，匹夫有责"的"家国情怀"。家是最小国，国是千万家，要深刻明白个人命运与国家命运紧密相连。你们十分幸运，身处一个伟大的时代，这个时代比历史上任何时期都更接近实现民族复兴的目标。所以，今日之中国需要你们成为担当有为的青年，而不是潜水围观的看客。你们要更多地关心国家、关心人民、关心世界，正如重大校歌所言"复兴民族兮，誓作前锋"，年轻的你们应当勇敢地走向前列，以家国情怀书写壮丽青春，以使命担当承载民族希望，迎向时代赋予青年"奋进者""开拓者""奉献者"的夺目荣光！

第二，头上有星空，脚下有行动。

"头上有星空"就是要有远大志向和理想。古人云："志不立，天下无可成之事。"所以，做人必先立志，而且只有把个人的理想与国家、民族的理想有机结合才不会失去实现理想的土壤。要"仰望星空"也要"脚踏实地"，没有实际行动，再好的理想都是无源之水、无本之木。为实现理想要锲而不舍、持之以恒、矢志不渝；要勤勤恳恳、踏踏实实，不游戏人生，不浪费时光。在丰富的课堂学习和实践活动中，学会学习、学会做事、学会做人，学会和谐共处、学会适应瞬息万变的世界。要注重内心修炼，培养健全人格，增强公民意识，坚守做人原则和道德准则，"扣好人生第一粒扣子"。

第三，眼里有世界，心中有宁静。

在这个信息化高度发达的时代，大学校园与社会的"围墙"已不复存在，社会的纷繁喧闹打破了宁静的校园。在社会发展的滚滚洪流中，我们很难也没有必要去避开真实的社会，应该以开放的姿态适应这种改变，享受科技给生活带来的便利，并运用快捷的手段去认识这个世界。需要我们注意的是，认知世界的碎片化所导致的思维取向的

mental state caused by the shallow manifestation of the living world is becoming a trend. Impetuosity unavoidably exists on campus. As college students, we should never allow ourselves to go with the flow, and we should seek an undisturbed silence for study instead. The true tranquility is not to avoid the noisy world but to calm yourself down. In this way, you will not be lost in the world, and with the pursuit of dreams, you will create a good study environment for yourself.

My dear students, as the saying goes that "The sun will rise illuminating the path and streams will enter into the ocean unleashing overwhelming power"[1], you are the future of Chongqing University. You must always adhere to the school motto of Endurance, Thrifty, Diligence and Patriotism. You must set great ambitions, read more, and make accomplishments guided by the spirit of Chongqing University.

Thank you!

---

1   Quoted from *Young China Said* written by Liang Qichao (1873-1929).

直观化正成为一种"流行"，生活世界的浅显化所导致的精神状态的平庸化正成为一种"潮流"，校园也难免有些浮躁。作为大学生，我们不能放任自己随波逐流，应该为学习寻求一份不受干扰的宁静。真正的宁静不是避开"车马喧嚣"，而是在心中"修篱种菊"。这样你们才能在纷呈世相中不迷失荒径，怀着对梦想的追求，把自己的心沉寂下来，给自己营造一个良好的学习环境。

同学们，"红日初升，其道大光。河出伏流，一泻汪洋"[1]。你们是重大的未来，承载着重大人的希望。你们要始终秉承"耐劳苦、尚俭朴、勤学业、爱国家"的校训，立青云之志、揽万卷之文、汲文明之华、成恢宏之业，让重大精神指引你们前进的方向！

谢谢大家！

1　引自梁启超（1873—1929）的《少年中国说》。

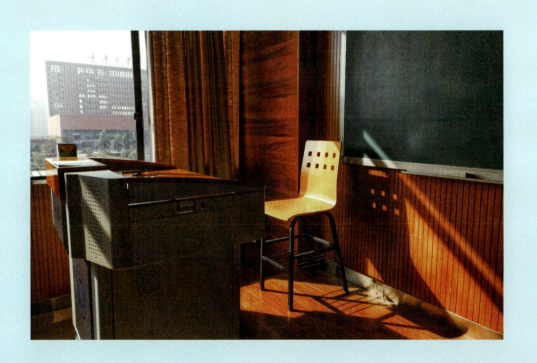

The Mind Required in Pursuit of Learning

—Speech at the Opening Ceremony of 2015 Graduate Students of Chongqing University

Dear students,

Good morning!

Chongqing University embraces fresh students every year when osmanthus flowers by the Democracy Lake are in full blossom. At the start of a new semester, the campus is filled with vitality with more than 4,600 fresh graduate students. On behalf of CQU, I would like to extend a warm welcome to you and congratulate you on your entering Chongqing University, where you will continue to explore science and human thoughts and open a new chapter of your life.

I would also like to thank you for your trust and love for CQU, a promising land of scholarship that deserves your trust and love. Since its founding in 1929, CQU has shown the world her endeavor in doing academic research, cultivating talents and enlightening the nation, and upholding the principle of dedicating to academic researches. For more than 80 years, CQU has adhered to her excellent traditions of running a university and ranked first in many scientific fields in China: the first 35-kilowatt short-wave radio station; the first gallic acid plastics in the history of Chinese chemical industry; Professor Feng Jian, the first Chinese scientist who completed the Arctic scientific expedition; Professor Le Senxun, the first scientist who discovered the ancient fish fossils of 300 million years ago; Professor Ding Daoheng, the first scientist who discovered the Baiyun Ebo iron ore mine;

做学问需要怎样的心境？

—— 在重庆大学 2015 级研究生开学典礼上的讲话

亲爱的同学们：

大家上午好！

每当民主湖畔桂树飘香，美丽的重大校园就会迎来新的面庞。又到一年开学季，由于 2015 级 4 600 余名研究生新同学的到来，校园里洋溢着盎然生机。首先，我代表学校对你们表示热烈的欢迎，也祝贺你们通过自己的努力，如愿进入重大这座学术的殿堂，在这里继续攀登人类思想与科学的高峰，开启人生又一新的篇章！

同时，也要感谢你们的信赖与钟爱，把优秀的自己"托付"给重大。重大是一块学术的热土，值得你们信赖。从 1929 年创办之时，重大就向世人庄严地宣告"研究学术、造就人才、佑启乡邦、振导社会"，并始终坚持把"研究学术"作为学校的立校之本和办学之基。八十多年来，秉承优良的办学传统，重大在学术研究的道路上创造了中国科学界的多项第一：成功创建了国内第一座 35 千瓦短波电台；成功研发了我国化工史上第一批棓酸塑料；冯简教授成为中国的北极

the first industrial CT machine successfully developed in China; the first National Invention Award of Chinese universities and the first State Science and Technology Prizes ... As the president of CQU and a supervisor of graduate students, I sincerely hope that you will commit yourselves to doing academic researches, be enlightened by wisdom, hone your mind and grow up under the guidance of by the spirit of CQU— "Endurance, Frugality, Diligence, Patriotism".

Every year at the opening ceremony of graduate students, "study" and "innovation" have remained the topics. I know that you have already passed the age of being preached, so I would like to share with you some of my personal feelings and experiences. The year before last year, I talked about how to pursue learning, and last year about the qualities required in pursuit of learning. Today, I want to talk about the mind required in pursuit of learning, that is, commitment together with contemplation and precipitation.

Firstly, immerse yourselves in study.

To immerse yourselves means to commit yourselves to studying. The quiet campus is inevitably bothered by impetuosity in an era of information. Mrs. Curie who made great achievements in science once said in *My Faith*, "Working in a quiet environment and living a simple life is what I have always pursued. In order to realize it, I have made every effort to protect the environment from being disturbed by worldly affairs and fame." Zhuge Liang said in *Letter to Expostulate with Son*, "This is a way of life for a man of virture: to cultivate his character by keeping a peaceful mind, and nourish his morality by living a frugal life. Only freedom from vanity can show one's lofty goal of life, and only peace of mind can help him achieve something lasting. To be talented, one must learn; and to learn, one must have a peaceful mind". It can be seen that, like cultivation, study also requires peace and meditation. The way to learn lies in buckling down with the inner peace that sublimates thoughts.

To immerse yourselves in study requires not only serene surroundings but also peace of mind. On the modern university campus, where the static scenes described in the poem made by Tao Yuanming, the great poet who lived in the middle of the Six Dynasties that "While picking asters neath the eastern fence, my gaze upon the southern mountain rests" are missing, we can instead entertain the peace within like Tao Yuanming. Sometimes, it is unrealistic and unnecessary for us to escape from the noisy world. Despite that a pure and quiet study environment no longer exists, with the pursuit of knowledge and a settled-down mind, we can still create favorable

科学考察第一人；乐森璕教授第一个发现了3亿年前古生物鱼类化石；丁道衡教授第一个发现了白云鄂博铁矿；成功研制了国内第一台工业CT机；获得中国高校第一个国家发明奖和第一个城市规划国家科技进步奖……作为校长和研究生导师，我热切期盼你们在这片学术热土上潜心耕耘，衷心希望你们在"耐劳苦、尚俭朴、勤学业、爱国家"的重大精神感召下得到学术的锻炼、智慧的启迪、心志的砥砺和人生的成长。

每年在研究生开学典礼上，我都会围绕"做学问"和"创新"的话题与同学们交流探讨。我知道，大家早就过了能被说教的年龄，所以，我更多的是想与大家分享我个人的一些感悟和体会。记得前年我和同学们探讨了"怎样做学问"，去年和同学们交流了"做学问需要怎样的精神品质"，今天我想以"沉心、沉思、沉淀"为题和大家谈谈"做学问需要怎样的心境"。

首先，要学会"沉心"。

"沉心"，就是沉心静气，沉下心来做学问。当今社会网络发达，信息传递飞速，生活节奏不断加快，人们也不停地追赶着潮流，已经进入了一个"有耳必闻窗外事"的时代，宁静的校园难免有几分浮躁。居里夫人在科学上取得了巨大成就，她在《我的信念》一文中说道："我永远追求安静的工作和简单的生活。为了实现这个理想，我竭力保持宁静的环境，以免受人事的干扰和盛名的渲染。"诸葛亮在他的《诫子书》中说道："夫君子之行，静以修身，俭以养德。非淡泊无以明志，非宁静无以致远。夫学须静也，才须学也。"由此可见，不仅"修身"需要静思反省，"求学"更需要一种宁静的心境和放松的心灵。**学问之道，唯有以内心的深潜才能成就思想的升华，不让你的思想"沉陷"。**

要内心的深潜，不但需要清静的环境，更需要保持自己清静的心

surroundings where we won't be disturbed by the noises that even linger around our ears. Whether someone is immersed or not can simply be known to himself. A quiet self enables you to be fully immersed in books so that the mind will be constantly sublimated and the scholarship improved.

To steep in study, staying away from vanity and cultivating your character come into concern. Those who are famous are tired of fame, and those who seek profits are driven out by profit. Study can't be impetuous, so you need to be patient if you do something enough, and it will work out. Success is what we accumulate. We should remember: Impetuousness is the "natural enemy" of innovation, and "academic misconduct" is the "cancer" of innovation. Any behavior with luck is a non-return road. If you have no desire for profit, you will be calm; if you are calm, you will be wise. Everything in the world is not one's own, but the peace of mind truly belongs to yourself.

Secondly, lose yourselves in thoughts.

Lose yourselves in thoughts independently, deeply and meticulously. Hu Shi said that scientific research is "making bold assumptions and being careful to verify them." Where does boldness come from? I believe that the answer is from meditation. Ancients figured that study begins with thinking, and thinking comes from doubt. Einstein also said, "Studying knowledge needs thinking again and again." Thinking is digesting and absorbing what is learned, the key to deepening and sublimating knowledge, and the catalyst that gives birth to ideas and enlightens thinking. To learn, you must be thoughtful and enlightened. **The way to learn rests with deep thinking that motivates your thoughts.**

To think deeply, you must have the ability to think independently. At present, we are in a highly-developed information society where more information is more easily accessible on the Internet. Also because of accessibility, a great number of people are reluctant to think independently, accepting all thrown to them. Therefore, everyone's cognitions become more and more convergent, and the initiative of personal thinking is reduced by the network in a certain sense. I am not denying the convenience brought by the Internet, just want students not to be slaves of the network, but to be the masters diligent in dialectical thinking, and using the Internet to create new ideas.

To think deeply, you must have the ability to think critically. Innovation can't be separated from criticism, which is the source of innovation. Einstein said,

态。现代大学校园，已经难觅"采菊东篱下，悠然见南山"的静景，但我们可以拥有陶渊明那种"问君何能尔？心远地自偏"的心境，保持一种内心的平和安静，让心灵超凡洒脱，自然会幽静邈远。有时，我们很难也没有必要躲开纷繁喧闹的世界，一个纯正安静的学习环境已不复存在。我们只有怀着对学问的追求，把自己的心沉寂下来，才能给自己营造一个良好的学习环境。只要守住心灵的安静，即使杂音绕耳，也会心不动，行不乱。一个人安静与否在于心灵，心灵的安静也只有自己知道。你能寻求安静的自己和属于自己的安静，就能徜徉书海，品味书香，吮吸着智慧的芳华，让思想不断升华，学问不断提升。

要内心的深潜，就要淡泊名利，涵养心性。为名者被名累，逐利者被利逐。做学问不能心浮气躁、急功近利，要有一份"功到自然成"的耐心和定力，"积土成山"才会"风雨兴焉"；"积水成渊"方能"蛟龙生焉"。潜龙在渊，卧薪尝胆，方成大器。我们要谨记：浮躁是创新的"天敌"，"学术不端"是创新的"毒瘤"，任何抱有侥幸心理的行为走上的都是一条不归路。无利欲则心静，心静则明朗。世间万物苟非吾之所有，唯宁静的心性真正属于自己。

其次，要学会"沉思"。

"沉思"，就是独立、认真、深入的思考。胡适说，科学研究就是"大胆假设，小心求证"。那么，"胆"从何来？我认为"胆"应该从"沉思"中来。古人云："学起于思，思源于疑。"爱因斯坦也说过："学习知识要善于思考，思考，再思考。"思考是知识消化、吸收的过程，是知识深化、升华的关键，是催生思想，启迪思维的酵母。学习要有所思、有所悟。**学问之道，唯有以思考的深邃才能成就思维的活跃，不让你的思维"沉寂"。**

要思考深邃，必须具有独立思考的能力。当前我们处于一个信

"Asking a question is often more important than solving one." Don't be bound by conclusions, and dare to question, to develop new fields and perspectives. Questioning is not a simple rejection, but to be justified. In academic debates, we must respect others, examine ourselves, and treat criticism and being criticized equally.

To think deeply, we must have the ability of comprehensive thinking. "Learning to use knowledge" is the realm that scholars should pursue. Not only learn the discipline, but also enable yourselves to have an interdisciplinary vision and thinking. In the current fashionable words, it is called "cross-border development". I hope you will master multidisciplinary theories and methods through study in the future academic path. Whether it is the intersection of fields or the reference of thinking, it will be of great help to your research.

Thirdly, arm yourselves with accumulation.

Arm yourselves with accumulation in study. Lu Xun noted that "No pains, no gains, and after a long period of time, from less to more, miracles can be created." Hua Luogeng also said, "Wisdom lies in study, genius in accumulation." It has been thought that achievements at 50 come from 18-year-old ambition and 30-year-long hard work. The acquisition of knowledge hinges on the accumulation and only with the accumulation of quantity will there be a qualitative leap. However, the real scholars, not only being good at accumulating professional knowledge, stand out for charm of personalities and loft visions of life, which are far more significant. **The way of study lies in the depth of accumulation that determines your improvement.**

Nobility reflected in behaviors is a must for being finely educated. Einstein once pointed out that in most people's opinions, it was intelligence that made a scientist but, in his opinion, it was nobility. I look at the way of study as the way of behaving for if a man can be diligent, rigorous and pragmatic in study, so must he be in behaving, and vice versa. We respect scientists due to their intelligence, as well as their nobility, broad minds and strong sense of responsibility and dedication to society, country and people particularly. Instructed by supervisors' words and deeds and rigorous academic training, you should foster a life attitude of being unwilling to mediocrity, unafraid of failure, and unstoppable in pursuing excellence; foster an enterprising spirit of hard struggle and perseverance; foster good qualities of unity and cooperation, honesty and trustworthiness; and foster professional ethnics of being unsparing in seeking perfection. Learn to study, learn to behave, and cultivate

息高度发达的社会，网上信息越来越多，获取信息越来越简单，也正因为这种"简单"，很多人不愿再去独立思考，不管正确与否，都照单全收、人云亦云，致使每个人的认知越来越趋同，个人思维的能动性在某种意义上被网络消减。我并非否定网络带来的便利，只是想让同学们不要做网络的奴隶，而要去做网络的主人，勤于思考、善于思考、辩证思考，利用网络去创造新的思想。

要思考深邃，必须具有批判思考的能力。创新离不开批判，批判是创新的源泉。爱因斯坦说："提出一个问题往往比解决一个问题更重要。"做研究不要受已有结论的束缚，要敢于质疑，敢于拓展新的领域和视角。质疑不是简单的拒绝，而是要有理有据。在学术争辩中也要尊重他人、审视自己，平等地对待批评和被批评。

要思考深邃，必须具有综合思考的能力。"学问观其会通"是学者应该追求的境界，不仅能在本学科领域融会贯通、博采众长，还要让自己具备跨学科的视野和思维，用现在时髦一点的话讲，叫"跨界发展"。我希望同学们在未来的学术道路上，通过学习努力掌握多学科的理论与方法，不管是领域的交叉，还是思维的借鉴，对你的研究都会大有帮助。

最后，要学会"沉淀"。

"沉淀"，就是学习的感悟和积淀。鲁迅说："有一分劳动就有一分收获。日积月累，从少到多，奇迹就可以创造出来。"华罗庚也说过："聪明在于学习，天才在于积累。"有人认为，50岁的成就来自18岁的志向和30年的血汗。知识的获得，在于点滴的积累、充实，有了量的积累才会有质的飞跃。但是，真正的大学问家，不只是善于积累专业知识，更重要的是他们的人格魅力和人生境界。**学问之道，唯有以积淀的深厚才能成就境界的提升，不让你的境界"沉沦"。**

要有深厚的学养，必须培养"为人"的品格。爱因斯坦说过一句

lofty aspirations to create a magnificent realm of life in the future.

Ways of acting are essentials for fine scholarship. What I mentioned above is how to do academic research, and many students may question that what if they do not live on it after graduation. Yes, you may not need to carve out a paper in the future, but you need academic research to develop your sense of innovation and the ability to adapt to the requirements of innovation; you may not need to invent a piece of equipment henceforth, but you need to cultivate your creative thinking and creative activities through academic research; you may not need to start a business, but you need to stimulate your passion and ability to start a business through academic research. I think no matter what career you are engaged in, awareness, thinking, passion and ability are urgently needed in the society, which is the true meaning of our "innovation and entrepreneurship education". So, after a lot of thinking and practice, you should sum up your methods of academic research. I believe that the "methodology" formed during the postgraduate period will benefit your outstanding achievement in the future.

My dear students, this year marks the 70th anniversary of the victory of the Chinese People's War of Resistance Against Japanese Aggression. We were deeply impressed by the military parade on the Victory Day on September 3. The two figures, 35 million casualties in the 14 years of the War of Resistance Against Japanese Aggression, remind us of the past and of cautioning the future risks. The War of Resistance Against Japanese Aggression has left a profound lesson for the Chinese people, that is, "if you fall behind, you must be beaten, and only by development can you become stronger." Today, the innovation ability is the core competitiveness of the country and the nation. The innovation drive has become the national development initiative. Only innovators can make great progress, can become stronger and can win outright victory. Each generation has its own stage and mission, and you should shoulder the responsibility of building an innovative country. Whether the country, society, or school has unlimited expectations for you. In the best years of your life, you have chosen Chongqing University as the "gas station" where your dreams set off. I hope that you will inherit and carry forward the great tradition of CQU, devote yourselves to making progress, achieve in your study, and accumulate more energy for the great rejuvenation of the Chinese nation.

Thank you!

话："大多数人都以为是才智成就了科学家，他们错了，是品格。"我认为，"为学"之道亦即"为人"之道，为学之勤、之严、之实，其为人也必勤、必严、必实；为学之浮躁，其为人也必是浮躁之人。我们敬重科学家，不仅是因为他们的才智，更因为他们高尚的品格、宽阔的心怀和对社会、国家、人民强烈的责任心和献身精神。我们要在导师的言传身教和严格的学术训练中，树立不甘平庸、不怕失败、追求卓越的人生态度，培育艰苦奋斗、锲而不舍的进取精神，培养团结协作、诚实守信的优良品质，锻炼爱岗敬业、精益求精的职业操守，修炼为学之道和为人之道，蓄养浩然之志气，开创未来恢宏的人生境界。

要积淀深厚的学养，必须学会"为事"的方法。前面我讲的都是做学问，可能有很多同学会说我毕业后未必从事学术研究。是的，也许你今后不需要"创新"一篇论文，但是我们需要通过学术研究来培养你创新的意识和适应创新要求的能力；也许你今后不需要"创造"一台设备，但是我们需要通过学术研究来培养你创造的思维和开展创造性活动的能力；也许你今后不用"创业"做一个老板，但是我们需要通过学术研究来培养你创业的激情和创业的能力。这些意识、思维、激情、能力，我想不管你今后从事什么职业，社会都是急迫需要的，这才是我们"创新创业教育"的真正内涵。所以，同学们要在大量的思考和实践之后，好好总结你们从事学术研究的方法，我相信在研究生阶段形成的"方法论"，将有益于你们未来取得杰出的成就。

同学们，今年是中国人民抗战胜利70周年，一周前"抗战胜利日"阅兵给我们留下了深刻的印象，尤其不能忘记的还有两个数字：抗日14年，军民伤亡3 500万。无论是时间的长度还是伤亡的程度，都足以让我们铭记历史、警示未来。抗日战争给中国人民留下了一条深刻的教训，那就是"落后就要挨打，发展才能自强"。当今时代，

创新能力就是国家和民族的核心竞争力，创新驱动已成为国家发展战略，唯创新者进，唯创新者强，唯创新者胜。一代人有一代人的舞台，一代人有一代人的使命，你们这代人理所当然应该肩负起创新型国家建设的重任，无论是国家、社会，还是学校，都对你们充满了无限的期待。在你们人生最美好的岁月，你们选择了重庆大学作为自己梦想启航的"加油站"，希望你们继承和发扬重大的优良传统，珍惜时光、沉潜精进、学有所成，为中华民族的伟大复兴蓄积更强能量、奏响更强乐章！

　　谢谢大家！

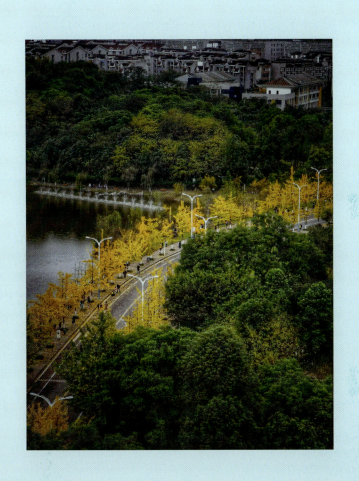

Youth Is a Rainbow That Never Fades Away

—Speech at the 2014 Graduation Ceremony of Chongqing University

Dear students,

It's time to bid farewell to you as Delonix regia flowers are in full blossom.[1] Strolling on the campus, you may feel some melancholy that you will soon say goodbye to the campus that records your youth. You may wonder "where time has gone"[2]; you may be a bit excited to plan and start a new journey towards your life full of possibilities. Fortunately, you can still have a zestful farewell dinner party on which you can voice your deep affection in toasting; you can stay up all night watching the World Cup[3] to drown your sorrows of parting; you can have a secret final dating with your beloved on the grassy Lover Slope[4]. What is more, you are so lucky to attend the most rained and as a result coolest graduation ceremony in the history of Chongqing University[5].

---

1 From the lyrics of a song "Delonix Regia Flowers Blooming Crossroad". This is a song about college graduation, quietly telling a story about youth, about growing up, and expressing a feeling of nostalgia.

2 From the song "Where Has Time Gone". On February 7, 2014, President Xi Jingping metioned this song when interviewed by Russian TV, which made it more popular.

3 From June 12 to July 13, in 2014, the 20th FIFA World Cup was being held in Brazil, coinciding with graduation season.

4 A scenic spot in Huxi campus of Chongqing University.

5 It was very hot in Chongqing in June, but on the morning of June 29, 2014, when the graduation ceremony was held, it rained heavily. Although the students were wearing raincoats, the rain brought them a little bit of coolness.

青春是一道永不落幕的彩虹

—— 在重庆大学 2014 届学生毕业典礼上的讲话

亲爱的同学们：

凤凰花开[1]，又到一年离别和欢送的时节。每当这个时候，校园里就激荡着一种复杂的情感。这几天，漫步在校园里，你可能有些许惆怅，亲近多年的菁菁校园即将与之分别，不由感叹"时间都去哪儿了"[2]；你也许还有一点"小兴奋"[3]，憧憬着未来拥有无尽可能的人生旅程，规划着自己"稳稳的幸福"[4]。还好，伴随着这种复杂的情感，我们有热火朝天的"散伙饭"，在推杯换盏间表达着你我的深情厚谊；有熬更守夜的"世界杯"[5]，在痛快欢呼中排解着彼此的离愁别绪；有绿草如茵的"情人坡"[6]，在卿卿我我中互道珍重。更让人意外的是，重大"史

1　凤凰花开——引自流行歌曲《凤凰花开的路口》，这是一首关于大学毕业离别的歌曲，轻声地诉说着一个关于青春、关于成长的故事，表达了对同学、老师、校园的一种不舍和留恋。
2　引自流行歌曲《时间都去哪儿了》。2014 年 2 月 7 日，国家主席习近平在接受俄罗斯电视台专访时，提到了春晚歌曲《时间都去哪儿了》，因此更加流行。
3　网络语言。
4　源自流行歌曲《稳稳的幸福》。
5　2014 年 6 月 12 日至 7 月 13 日，2014 年第 20 届世界杯足球赛在巴西举行，正好与毕业季重合。
6　重庆大学虎溪校区景点名称。

On behalf of CQU, I would like to extend my heartfelt congratulations to you on your successful and honorable graduation. I would also like to invite you to join me in extending your gratitude to your teachers, classmates, friends and families for their help and support.

It's a season of both graduation and harvest. CQU with a profound culture records your unforgotten memories and gives you the most valuable wealth of life. You have all grown into ambitious young people from awkward and naive freshmen like butterflies winging from cocoons. Here you have acquired knowledge, bettered wisdom and cultivated personalities, leaving your footsteps of self-improvement. Your bond with your alma mater will always be the most important part of your life. From today on, you will be alumni instead of students of CQU, but still continuing to carry on and practice the spirit of CQU with your personalities, values and power obtained here that will help you approach your life goals. In other words, your future is connected with that of Chongqing University.

My dear students, your alma mater is a station on the road to a beautiful life, where you will leave and face new life and challenges. The reason why we are nostalgic for our university is that our most brilliant youth was recorded here. The graduation season is the youth season. When talking about youth, it seems that there is always a trace of nostalgia because graduation seems to mean that youth is gradually far away. The movie *So Young* has set off a wave of reminiscences of youth. But I thought that the university time only passed away but your youth is a rainbow that never fades away.

Time of youth on campus is beautiful for its purity and otherworldly holiness; it is proud with a firmly belief that "there must a use for my talent"; it is enthusiastic with the quality of promoting the good and abandoning the evil; it is brave without fearing others' views and the bumpy road ahead; it is ideal with a passion of regarding the national affairs as their own duty. Regret that youth is fleeting, in fact, not because of the passing times but the aged mood. In a sense, there is no connection between youth and age; some young people have a withered mind while some aged people still have great ambitions. Years only change your appearance, but if you abandon the time of youth, your mind will be covered with dust. In fact, youth is not the time that has passed, but a positive attitude.

Then, what kinds of attitudes represent youth? It is the listening of inner heart, the passion of pursuing wonderfulness, the persistence of chasing the dream,

上最凉快的毕业季"[1]居然被你们遇上，同窗的情谊伴随着这份清凉，你们也要且行且珍惜！

此时此刻，你们沐浴着毕业的荣耀和喜悦，我代表学校向你们表示衷心的祝贺！在这重要和激动的时刻，也请你们和我一道，感谢这一路帮助你们走来的老师、同学、朋友和家人！

岁月静好，似水流年，转眼又是毕业季。毕业季即收获季，在这所底蕴深厚的学府里，记录了你们太多值得回忆的青春故事，你们也收获了人生最宝贵的财富。几年前，你们还是局促不安的懵懂新生，现在破茧成蝶般、业已成为意气风发的阳光青年。你们在这里接受了知识的洗礼、智慧的启迪和人格的熏陶，也留下了奋进的足迹。你们与母校结下的不解情缘将永远成为生命中最重要的一部分。从今天开始，你们将完成"学生"到"校友"的转变，和以往所有重大的毕业生一样，将永远打上"重大人"的烙印，共同承载起"耐劳苦、尚俭朴、勤学业、爱国家"的文化符号，深切感受重大文化赋予你的品格、价值和力量，帮助你走近人生的梦想。你们的未来就是重大的未来！

同学们，母校是美丽人生路上的一处驿站，你们终将离开这里去面对新的生活和新的挑战。大学之所以让我们这般留恋和回味，是因为这里记载着我们最灿烂的青春年华。毕业季即青春季，谈及青春，好像总有那么一丝留恋，因为毕业似乎意味着青春渐行渐远。电影《致我们终将逝去的青春》掀起了一股青春怀旧的热潮，正是切中了"青春散场"[2]的心理。但我以为，终将逝去的只是大学时光，青春不会随着毕业而消逝，你们的青春是一道永不落幕的彩虹！

1　6月的重庆十分炎热，但2014年6月29日上午举行毕业典礼时，天下起了大雨，同学们虽然都穿着雨披，却感受到几分凉爽。
2　《青春散场》是一首流行歌曲，歌词带着一种青春逝去、朋友分别的落寞感伤。

the independent personality that dares to criticize, and the social responsibility of "Every man alive has a duty to his country". After graduation, as you enter the world of adult, your minds will gradually mature. But "being mature" does not mean becoming sophisticated or the passage of youth. In a complicated society where you may encounter many life choices, the mentality of "youth" and the courage to be young should be always kept. I hope that you can always keep a youthful mind.

Keeping a youthful heart allows you to truly recognize yourself.

To quote a line from *Lao Zi*, "It is valuable for and wise of one to know oneself." The most important thing for a person is self-knowledge. Many people fail not because they are not good, but because they don't know themselves correctly and don't know their goals and pursuits. On this question, we instinctively hope to find an answer and hope someone can tell us what we should do with our lives, but no one can. Everyone's life calls their own, and their own questions should be answered by themselves.

Time of youth is pure full of ideals. By maintaining a youthful mindset, we can listen to our true inner voices in purity, position ourselves in our ideals, find the right direction, cherish our talents and give full play to our strengths. If a sleek person mocks that you are not "mature" or a smart person thinks that you are not wise, please don't be afraid and try not to mind, because you don't have to imitate the so-called success model of others, but choose to listen to your own inner call and be the best self!

Keeping a youthful heart can make you optimistic and stick to your dreams.

"No beginning, no ending."[1] It is easy to build a dream, but difficult to pursue it. We live in an era of profound changes. Due to rapid development of the Internet, new things are springing. The complexity of market economy makes all sorts of ideological trends emerge ceaselessly. When the thoughts of utility and impetuosity invade the pure land dubbed as dream, can the gorgeous dream resist the disintegration of "concreteness and triviality", and can the ambition endure the consumption of "mediocrity"?

Youth is tough, but also full of passion and creativity. As long as a youthful mindset is maintained, we have the strong will, perseverance and optimistic

---

1   Quoted from *The Book of Songs*, which means that few of people who do things with a good beginning would finish them well.

校园的青春之所以美好，因为它是纯真的，有着"不食人间烟火"的圣洁；它是骄傲的，坚信"天生我材必有用"的信念；它是热情的，有着扬善弃恶的品质；它是勇敢的，毫不畏惧别人的眼光和前路的风险坎坷；它是理想的，总有一份以天下为己任的豪情万丈。感慨青春易逝，其实更多的不是因为年华已老，而是心境已不似当年。从某种意义上讲，青春与年龄无关，有些人年纪尚轻，但心灵已经枯萎；有些人虽然已是伏枥老骥，却仍然志在千里。岁月催生的只是皱纹，但你若放弃青春，心灵就会布满灰尘。其实，青春不是逝者如斯的年华，而是积极向上的心态。

那么，青春是怎样的一种态度？它是遵从内心的真实倾听，是憧憬美好的激情燃烧，是追逐梦想的执着坚守，是勇于批判的独立人格，是"天下兴亡，匹夫有责"的社会担当。同学们毕业走向社会，从此进入成人的世界，心智将会逐渐成熟。但"成熟"不等于磨去棱角，不等于平庸世故，不等于青春的夭亡。身处纷繁复杂的社会，面对众多的人生抉择，"青春"的心态不应老去，"年轻"的勇气不应丧失，我希望同学们永葆一颗年轻的心，让"青春"常驻心间。

保持一颗青春的心，能让你真实地认知自我。

"人贵自知，自知者明。"一个人最重要的是对自我的认知，很多人失败不是因为不优秀，而是对自己认知不正确，不知道自己的目标和追求。在这个问题上，我们本能地希望能找到现成的答案，希望有人能直接告诉自己应该怎样去生活，但没有人能告诉我们。每个人的生活都是自己的，自己的问题应该由自己来回答。

青春是单纯的，也是富有理想的。保持青春的心态，我们就能在单纯中倾听自己内心真实的声音，在理想中定位最真实的自己，从而找准方向，珍惜天赋，发挥特长。如果圆滑的人笑话你不够"成熟"，如果聪明的人认为你不够明智，请你不用害怕和在意，你大可不必去

and positive attitude to achieve our dreams. Youth is also brave and proud. So entertaining a youthful mindset is having the courage to criticize and to abandon the drift, to be away from being manipulated by others, by fame and by desire. We will be able to achieve self-possession, self-confidence and self-motivation. Don't forget your original intention so that you can get the result you want in the end.

Keeping a youthful heart can make you assume the social responsibility you deserve.

"For the purpose of the national benefits, everyone is obligated to sacrifice themselves rather than escape from the misfortune for their own benefits." If we never shy away from difficulties and dare to take responsibility, our country and our nation will have a bright future. In a period of transition, there are interwoven social contradictions and complex multi-culture in today's society. Once you leave the campus, you may encounter more doubts and more immoral things like that: If an old man fell to the ground, should we help him or not? If something unfair happened, should we offer help or not? If we met a beggar, should we help him? Would you believe what the media clarified or not? If we met charity events, should we donate or not? These are simple questions in class, but now we are conflicted.

Youth is full of passion as well as the sense of justice. By maintaining a youthful attitude, we can stick to our beliefs, distinguish between right and wrong, stay away from fraud and sin, and go out of mediocrity and narrowness. Although the social condition is not satisfactory, the public's conscience and the bottom line of society still guard the goodness. As graduate students of Chongqing University, all of you will become the mainstay of society. We must shoulder the social responsibility that "everyone should be responsible for the prosperity of the country" and carry forward the morality in society. As the president, I don't require all students to become social elites, but I hope that all of you can become patriotic, law-abiding, honest and courteous modern citizens, who are respectable in society, trustworthy in your posts and reliable in your families. I don't require you all to be dignitaries, but I hope that you will have a complete personality and a happy life!

Dear students, it's time to say goodbye. Standing here, I am like a farewell elder wishing you a smooth sailing life. In the future, no matter who you are, the alma mater with open arms welcomes all of you to come back for a visit, to share the joy of success and to resolve the sorrows in your heart. I believe that what the alma mater gives to you, in addition to the good memories, are endless motivation, firm beliefs

效仿他人所谓的成功范本，而应选择倾听自己内心的呼唤，做你最好的自己！

保持一颗青春的心，能让你乐观坚守梦想。

"靡不有初，鲜克有终。"[1] 筑梦易，追梦难，实现梦想需要坚强的意志和执着的坚守。我们生活在一个深刻变革的时代，互联网的飞速发展，使得新生事物如雨后春笋般层出不穷；市场经济的泥沙俱下，使各种思潮不断涌现。当功利、浮躁等思想逐渐侵扰"梦想"这块净土，梦想的绚烂是否能抵抗住"具体琐碎"的消解，万丈雄心是否能承受"平庸世故"的消磨？

青春是坚韧的，也是富有激情和创造的。保持青春的心态，我们就具备了实现梦想所需要的坚强意志、执着坚守和乐观积极的态度。青春也是勇敢和骄傲的，保持青春的心态，我们就会勇于批判，摈弃随波逐流，不受他人摆布，不做功名的奴隶，不做欲望的俘虏，就能做到稳重自持、从容自信、坚定自励，不忘初心，方得始终！

保持一颗青春的心，能让你承担起应有的社会担当。

"苟利国家生死以，岂因祸福避趋之"，事不避难，敢于担当，国家就有前途，民族就有希望。我国社会正处于转型期，各种社会矛盾相互交织，多元文化错综并呈。走出校园，你们可能会遇到更多的疑惑，可能碰到更多的"三观尽毁""节操尽碎"[2]。老人倒地扶不扶？路见不平吼不吼？乞丐伸手给不给？媒体澄清信不信？爱心捐款捐不捐？……这些曾经在"思想品德"课中再简单不过的问题，现在都让我们纠结于心。

青春是热情的，也是富有正义感的。保持青春的心态，我们就能

1　这是《诗经》中的一句话，意思是说人们做事大都有一个良好的开端，但很少有人能够善始善终。
2　网络常见用词。泛指那些颠覆世界观、人生观和价值观，破坏了气节、操行，丧失原则、道德的人和事。

and a source of happiness.

I recall a song, "When the buttercups burst again, ..., on the covered hillside, at the crossroads ..., I say goodbye to the friends I cherish most." Goodbye, my dear students.

I wish you peace and happiness!

坚守自己的信仰，明辨是非、扬善弃恶，远离欺诈与罪恶，走出平庸与狭隘。社会虽然不尽如人意，但大众的良知和社会的底线仍然守护着善良。作为重大的毕业生，必将成为社会的中流砥柱，我们要肩负起"天下兴亡，匹夫有责"的社会担当，在社会中引领道德风尚。作为校长，我不求我的学生人人都成为社会精英，但我希望你们人人都能成为爱国、守法、诚信、知礼的现代公民，在社会上赢得尊重，在岗位上值得信任，在家庭里可以依靠。我不求你们个个"达官显贵"，但希望你们人格完整、生活如意、幸福安康！

同学们，就要和你们说再见了。站在这里，我就像一位送行的长者驻足凝望，盼望你们一帆风顺，一生幸福。今后，不管你正值春风得意居庙堂之高，还是等待厚积薄发处江湖之远，母校都欢迎你们回来看看。母校将以博大的胸怀迎接你们，和你们一起分享成功的喜悦，一起排解心中的忧愁。我相信，母校给予你们的，除了美好的回忆，还有不竭的动力、坚定的信念和快乐的源泉！

我想起一首歌，"又到凤凰花开放的时候，……，染红的山坡，道别的路口，……，有我最珍惜的朋友"——同学们，再见！

祝你们平安、快乐、幸福！

Your University, Your Stage

—Speech at the Opening Ceremony of 2014 Undergraduates of Chongqing University

Dear students,

Today, the beautiful Huxi campus is receiving new vitality. Your arrival has injected fresh blood into Chongqing University and making her more vigorous. CQU school song says, "Select outstanding talents from various places to become students of CQU, and these students have national integrity and patriotic feelings." [1] Years of hard work bring you to CQU that you've always dreamed of. I am sincerely proud of you, and that CQU has gathered so many talents all over the country. On behalf of all the teachers and students, I would like to welcome all of you to join us and look forward to your pursuit of higher dreams in life!

Some of you might find the past summer vacation a little "long". Since the day you got the admission notice, you have been longing for the moment when "I meet you in CQU" and for "the growth by the Jialing River". [2] Having waited for such a long time, today we finally meet here. You must be very excited when first setting foot on this land because the city of lush mountains and lucid rivers is not surrounded by the mist and the picturesque and lively Huxi campus is not as venerable as you imagined. You may not expect that this city, this school, and the people here will be

---

1 Quoted from the school song of Chongqing University.
2 Quoted from the inscription of Wu Guanzhong, a famous contemporary painter and art educator.

你的大学，你的舞台

—— 在重庆大学 2014 级本科生开学典礼上的讲话

亲爱的同学们：

今天美丽的虎溪校园又迎来了朝气蓬勃的新生力量，你们的到来为重庆大学注入了新鲜的血液，使今日重大更加生机盎然、英姿勃发。重大校歌有言，"考四海而为俊，障百川而之东"[1]，你们经过多年的奋斗，在求学路上脱颖而出，来到了梦寐以求的大学，看着你们青春洋溢的笑脸，意气风发的神情，我由衷地为你们感到骄傲，我也为重大"得天下英才而育之"感到自豪。在这里，我代表重庆大学全体师生员工，欢迎各位新"重大人"的"倾情加盟"，期待你们追寻人生更高的梦想！

刚刚过去的暑假，对于你们来说，可能在期盼中感觉有些"漫长"。从拿到录取通知书的那天起，就一天天地憧憬着"如果在重大

1　引自《重庆大学校歌》。"考四海而为俊"的意思是聚天下英才而育之；"障百川而之东"出自韩愈《进学解》中的"障百川而东之，回狂澜于既倒"，意思是阻挡千百条江河使之向东流去，把汹涌的波涛挽转回来，寓意教育学生使之成才。

closely linked to your future and will remain so for the rest of your lives.

As freshmen, you are full of excitement and pride, just like the poem describes that "Galloping on the crest of wave and in the spring wind, I appreciate flowers in Chang'an within one day". You are excited about college life and do not know where to start. There is a famous saying in the West, "A good beginning is half done"; our ancient people also said, "A road of a thousand miles begins with one step". When you first arrive at the university, the first question you face is how to take the first step well. Only when you understand what a university is and what she can bring to you will you make a scientific plan for your future, so that you don't have to be a "hurried passenger" in university. I think this is the most important topic that I, as president, should talk to you at the opening ceremony.

What is a university? The *Great Learning* on the wall of Confucius Square on our Huxi campus gives a clear description, "The way of great learning consists in manifesting one's bright virtue, consists in loving the people, consists in stopping in perfect goodness." I think the way of learning is consistent to that of today. The lifestyle of "investigating things, extending knowledge, making their wills sincere, correcting their minds, cultivating themselves, harmonizing their own clan, governing well their states, and making peace throughout the land" suggested by the *Great Learning* is supposed to be the dream and pursuit of universities.

The university is not only a place for teaching knowledge. The greatness of a university, in spite of that she is a palace of knowledge, reflects in that she is the carrier of civilization, a symbol of the spirit of the times, a beacon of social fashion and a spiritual home of mankind. A good university must be a university with a soul that is the unique tradition, culture and spirit of the university. Chongqing University, founded in 1929, came into being in the era of saving the nation. Soon after the establishment of the university, Chongqing served as a wartime capital with a large pool of talents and great masters. In the 1940s, she developed into one of the ten national universities with the most complete disciplines and the most comprehensive strength in China, laying a fine university-running tradition and profound cultural foundation for the development of the university. For eighty-five years since the founding of the school, we have persisted "the cultivation of talents, the study of scholarship, helping the development of the hometown and mobilizing the society" as our own duty, and have held on to the dream of "building a complete and profound university". The university has been established in difficult and

遇见你"的韶华时光，向往着"嘉陵江畔度青春"[1]的历练成长，等待了这么久，今天我们终于在重大相遇。初次踏上这片土地，心情肯定无比激动，山水之城没有传说中的氤氲雾绕，而是山明水晰、错落有致；虎溪校园也没有想象中的那样森严老成，而是风景如画、灵动朝气。你们可能未曾预料，这座城市，这所学校，这里的人们，将与你们的未来紧紧相连、情牵一生。

刚刚进入大学的你们，既充满了激动，也充满了豪情，可谓"春风得意马蹄疾"，所以想着"一日看尽长安花"，对大学生活跃跃欲试，但又不知从何做起。西方有句名言，"好的开始，等于成功了一半"；我们古人也讲，"千里之行，始于足下"。初到大学，你们面临的首要问题是如何迈好第一步。只有明白了什么是大学，大学能给你带来什么，你们才能为自己的未来做好科学的规划，才不至于在大学里做一名"匆匆过客"。我想，这是我作为校长在开学典礼上最应该给你们谈的话题。

什么是大学？在我们虎溪校区孔子广场的《大学》文化墙上这样开宗明义："大学之道，在明明德，在亲民，在止于至善。"虽然这里的《大学》并非我们今天所讲的大学，但我认为其内涵是一致的。《大学》所推崇的"格物、致知、诚意、正心、修身、齐家、治国、平天下"的人生境界，理应成为我们大学的理想和情怀。

大学并非只是传授知识的场所，大学之所以为"大"，因为她不仅是知识的殿堂，还是传承文明的载体、时代精神的象征、社会风尚的灯塔、人类的精神家园。一所好的大学一定是有灵魂的大学。所谓灵魂，就是一所大学独特的传统、文化和精神。重庆大学创办于

---

1 引自当代著名画家、美术教育家吴冠中题词。1942 年，吴冠中于国立杭州艺术专科学校毕业后，任重庆大学建筑系助教。吴冠中说重庆是他的福地，青春与爱情都在此闪光。于是他带着深厚的感情于2002 年新春时节为嘉陵江畔的岁月留下题词："蜀中忆，最忆是重庆，嘉陵江畔度青春"。而今吴冠中题词的雕塑位于重庆大学 B 校区第二综合楼前。

tortuous circumstances. After the adjustment of departments, she was integrated into a comprehensive university, joining both "211 Project" and "985 Project" with great efforts and refining our school motto of "Endurance, Thrifty, Diligence, Patriotism". This spirit is rooted in the unpretentious and unpretentious folk customs of the Bayu region that has the same origin with the indomitable spirit of Hongyan Spirit, just like the Huangge trees on campus that will still hold their heads up to the wind and strive to thrive and offer cool places even though situated on a cliff. What CQU embodies is the patriotic spirit of rejuvenating the Chinese nation, the scientific spirit of pursuing truth, hard-working spirit, the spirit of the times to be innovative. Under the great spirit, she cultivated batches of outstanding alumni, contributing significantly to national independence and liberation, motherland prosperity and human progress.

Students not only gain knowledge in university, but also learn how to behave. Mr. Cao Yunxiang[1], a well-known educator, said, "The so-called university is not just dedicated to teaching reciting and memorizing. She is intended to develop a noble and complete personality and prepare students for a social foothold." Therefore, I believe that a university is to nourish students with knowledge and cultivate their minds, that is, the acquisition of knowledge and the formation of personality. A good university education can endow students with truth of being a person, the skill of study, and the ability of doing things. However, to achieve the best educational effect, schools and students need to work together!

Chongqing University has always regarded nurturing talents as her most fundamental mission and the provision of the best education for students as her most important responsibility. Mr. Cai Yuanpei said, "Education is to help the educated to develop their abilities and complete their personalities, not to make the educated a special instrument." For a long time, focusing on the fundamental task of "strengthening moral education and cultivating people", CQU has adhered to the principle of "educating people first", and strived to provide a free, open and diversified educational environment for students to inspire their wisdom; has cultivated innovative spirit, and helped them establish right outlook on life and values to distinguish between right and wrong and pay attention to society and be kind to others with a sense of responsibility; has helped them further achieve all-

---

1   Cao Yunxiang (1881-1937), the fifth president of Tsinghua University between 1922 and 1928.

1929 年，在救国图存的时代呼唤中应运而生。建校不久，借重庆作为战时陪都之利，人才荟萃，大师云集，在 20 世纪 40 年代重大就发展成为当时中国学科门类最为齐全、综合实力最为雄厚的十所国立大学之一，为学校发展奠定了优良的办学传统和深厚的文化底蕴。建校八十五年来，重大坚持以"研究学术、造就人才、佑启乡邦、振导社会"为己任，胸怀"建完备弘深之大学"的梦想，在困难曲折中艰难创办，历战火纷飞，经院系调整，从单科性恢复综合性，从"211"到"985"……，励精图治，踔厉前行，锤炼出"耐劳苦、尚俭朴、勤学业、爱国家"的重大精神。她根植于巴渝大地朴实无华的淳朴民风，与山城儿女顽强不屈的"红岩精神"同脉相承，正如重大校园里的黄葛树，即使置身于悬崖峭壁，也迎风昂首，奋力茁壮，一半沐浴阳光，一半洒落阴凉。她体现的是振兴中华，匹夫有责的爱国精神，崇尚学术、追求真理的科学精神，勤俭办学、吃苦耐劳的奋斗精神，锐意改革、勇于创新的时代精神。在重大精神的感召下，这里培育出了一批批杰出的校友，为民族独立、人民解放、祖国繁荣和人类进步做出了不可磨灭的贡献！

学生在大学里不仅获得知识，更重要的是懂得做人做事的道理。著名教育家曹云祥先生[1]说："所谓大学，并非专事诵读记忆而已，是欲养成高尚完全之人格，为立足社会之准备。"所以，我认为：大学之于学生，一是滋养学识，二是涵养心灵，即知识的获得和人格的养成；良好的大学教育能赋予学生做人的"本真"、学习的"本事"和做事的"本领"。然而，实现最好的教育效果，需要学校和学生的共同努力！

重庆大学始终把"造就人才"作为最根本的使命，把为学生提供最好的教育当作最重要的责任。蔡元培先生讲："教育是帮助被教育

1　曹云祥（1881—1937），1922—1928 年任清华学校第五任校长。

round development in knowledge, ability and quality, and grow into society's pillars and backbone. No matter in the past or now, at home or abroad, no matter where you go, you can see alumni of Chongqing University struggling with loyalty and dedication to the country, the nation and humankind.

How to integrate into university life? The British thinker Whitehead said a century ago, "In the middle school stage, in terms of intellectual development, students remain at their desks and concentrate on their studies, while in university they should stand up and look around."[1] Learning to be self-determined is the prerequisite and end-result of university life. In fact, the university is your stage on which you are both a director and a protagonist dominating your colorful life programs. The university provides students with facilities, conditions, resources and platforms, which are equal to everyone. You are in a self-service education environment. You have to rely on your own design to obtain a good university education. Here, you must learn to think independently, to plan your future, to learn automatically, to be your own teacher, and to actively develop yourself and improve yourself. In a few years, you will all get a diploma, but for different university life, however, this diploma varies in meaning and value, which are directly proportional to your proactive efforts and struggles.

Firstly, you should take the initiative to practice, forming your fundamentals of life.

The university integrates the innocence of the middle school age and the principles of establishing yourselves outside school, including all kinds of things in the world. In face of various temptations that linger like dust, we are supposed to keep inner peace and inner cultivation; to cultivate healthy personalities, adhering to the principle of being human and the bottom line of morality; to establish an optimistic attitude; to learn to be grateful, and to know how to return; to be more tolerant, less cynical; to respect others, appreciate others, value friendship, be good at cooperation, and pay attention to integrity; to be sensible and fair; to dare to dream and be willing to pursue; to believe God rewards those who work hard. Don't exaggerate your accomplishments and don't seek fame and fortune ... Look upon those who conduct nobly and study assiduously as a mountain peak and act in accordance with their behaviors as a code, even though you can't achieve

1   Quoted from *The Aims of Education* written by Whitehead.

的人给他能够发展自己的能力，完成他的人格，不是把被教育的人造成一种特别的器具。"长期以来，重庆大学紧紧围绕"立德树人"这个根本任务，坚持"育人为本"，努力为学生发展提供自由、开放、多元的教育环境，通过滋养学识、陶冶情操，最大限度地启迪学生智慧、培育学生创新精神，帮助学生树立正确的人生观和价值观，教会学生明辨是非、勇于担当、关注社会、善待他人，在知识、能力、素质上得到全方位的发展，把学生造就成未来社会的栋梁之材和中坚力量。无论是过去还是现在，无论是国内还是国外，无论大江南北、五湖四海，无论你走到哪里，都能看到重大人奋斗的足迹和身影，感受到重大人对国家、对民族、对人类的忠诚和奉献。

究竟怎样融入大学生活？英国思想家怀特海在一个世纪前就说过："在中学阶段，从智力培养方面来说，学生们一直伏案专心于自己的课业；而在大学里，他们应该站立起来并环顾四周。"[1]学会自己做主是大学生活的前提和归宿。实际上，大学是一个舞台，一个属于你自己的舞台，在这里你既是导演也是主角，精彩的人生节目由你自己主宰。大学为学生提供了设施、条件、资源和平台，人人平等，你面对的是一个自助式的教育环境，要靠自己去设计才能获得良好的大学教育。在这里，你要学会独立思考、学会规划自我、学会自主学习、学会做自己的老师，要积极主动地去发展自我、完善自我。几年后，你们大都能得到一纸文凭，但对于不同的大学生活，这张文凭的意义和价值却大不相同，其含金量与你积极主动的努力和奋斗成正比。

第一，你要主动历练，形成自己做人的"本真"。

大学校园融入了中学时代的纯真，也融入了天南地北与社会方圆，包罗了世间百态、人间万象。面对种种如灰尘般挥之不去的诱

---

1 引自怀特海《教育的目的》一书。

this degree.

The Roots of Wisdom says, "The article to the extreme, there is no other strange, just right; personality to the extreme, no other different, just natural." The true person needs the depth and soul of thought. It is necessary to abandon greed and delusion, remove the mask and disguise, and stay away from the current wind and worldly customs. It is necessary to be simple, natural, honest and kind. This is the most precious quality of our life, work, and study. Only the true person can stand the torture of the inner heart and the test of time. Healthy and genuine personality can fill the gap of knowledge, while rich knowledge can hardly fill the defect of personality. Only when one can succeed in conducting oneself, can one succeed in doing things.

Secondly, you must take the initiative to learn, upgrading your abilities of study.

How should college students learn? The modern poet Wang Guowei gave a vivid and wonderful answer. He said, "Those who have accomplished great things in ancient and modern times will have to go through three levels of state. 'Start with the most basic book and work your way up' is the first level; 'When reading must be dedicated, to be willing to endure hardship' is the second level; 'There is pain and pleasure in reading, and enjoy the process' is the third level." In other words, to do a good job in study, you must have lofty ideals, clear goals, persistent pursuit, firm self-confidence and strong perseverance, and must be able to withstand loneliness. Only after hard work and without regrets can we gain the joy of success and realize our own ideals. If there is no spirit of sacrifice to go forward, indomitable perseverance, and self-confidence, study would not be done well.

The most basic task of college students is to study. You must set a great ambition, which is the driver of study; must work hard, which is the premise of study; must be content with loneliness, which is a kind of study mentality; and must show great perseverance, which is the foundation of study. You should set up the great ideal of study for the rejuvenation of the Chinese nation and persevere unswervingly in order to realize the ideal. You must be diligent and down-to-earth away from flirting with lives and away from pursuing fame and wealth. In study, you should overcome difficulties and build up firm confidence. Do not use improper means to gain good reputation and honor. You should be sensitive and eager to learn, and always ask questions.

Thirdly, you must take the initiative to attempt, cultivating your capabilities of

惑，要做到心如止水，不为所动；要注重内心修炼，培养健康人格，坚守做人原则和道德底线；要树立乐观向上的心态，坦然面对生活中的不愉快；要学会感恩，懂得回报；要多一些宽容，少一些愤世嫉俗；要尊重他人，欣赏他人，重情谊，善合作，讲诚信；要知书达理，不卑不亢；要敢于梦想，乐于追求；相信天道酬勤，功不唐捐。不"夸逞功业，炫耀文章"、追名逐利……如此高山仰止，景行行止；虽不能至，然心向往之。

《菜根谭》上说："文章做到极处，无有他奇，只是恰好；人品做到极处，无有他异，只是本然。"本真做人需要的是思想的精深和灵魂的感悟，需要摒弃贪欲和妄想、卸掉面具和伪装、远离时风和世俗，需要崇尚返璞归真，守住心灵的纯朴、自然、厚道和善良。本真是我们做人、做事、做学问最珍贵的品质，只有本真做人，才经得起内心的拷问和时间的检验。健康本真的人格能弥补知识的空白，但丰富的知识却难以填补人格的缺陷。只有做人成功，才能做事成功。

第二，你要主动学习，提高自己学习的"本事"。

大学生应该怎样学习？近代词人王国维做了生动精彩的回答，他说："古今之成大事业、大学问者，必经过三种之境界，'昨夜西风凋碧树，独上高楼，望尽天涯路'此第一境也。'衣带渐宽终不悔，为伊消得人憔悴'此第二境也。'众里寻他千百度，蓦然回首，那人却在，灯火阑珊处'此第三境也。"也就是说，要做好学问、成就一番事业，必须有远大的理想、明确的目标、执着的追求、坚定的自信和坚强的毅力，必须耐得住寂寞与孤独。只有经历过艰苦的努力，无怨无悔的追求，才能收获成功的喜悦，才能实现自己的理想。如果没有勇往直前的牺牲精神，没有坚韧不拔、百折不挠的毅力，没有必胜的自信心，学问是做不好的。

大学生最基本的任务就是学习。你们要立下鸿鹄之志，这是学

doing things .

If you only gain knowledge through books in college, it is a narrow way to accept university education, and improving abilities and qualities is the more important part of university education. There are many ways, from students' organizations, such as the Students' Union, the Association for Science and Technology, to student clubs of all kinds at all levels. Under the premise of ensuring study efficiency, you should take the initiative to grasp various training opportunities and participate in some public service activities, professional competitions and sports activities, social practice and professional practice activities, interpersonal interactions and community activities; you can also combine your own interests with majors, joining the scientific research team of the tutor. You can expand your circle of friends, get to know all kinds of outstanding students, and gain sincere friendship. You can also develop your communication and expression skills, leadership and coordination skills, practical and innovative abilities, and develop your own interests and broaden your horizons of development so as to enhance your overall quality and lay the foundation for future employment, entrepreneurship, as well as for further study.

Dear students, college life is a book whose title page has been turned over. I only write a prologue for you today, and the wonderful chapters still need to be written and completed by yourselves. I hope that you will be happy for the harvest and progress you are going to make every day. Let the buds of youth bloom here with beautiful dreams. I wish you sound personalities, serenity in mind and splendid achievements in study!

Tomorrow, you will start your military training which is a glorious tradition of CQU. You should be strict in self-discipline, and obey the command and orders. You should learn the good ideas and lifestyle of the army. You must respect the instructors, learn with humility, train assiduously and hone your qualities. In next month, we will be celebrating the 85th anniversary of Chongqing University, and we hope you will present a wonderful performance.

On behalf of the university, I would also like to express our sincere thanks and highest respect to the officers and soldiers who have accepted our freshmen's military training! I wish the military training a complete success!

Thank you!

习的动力所在；要勤奋努力，这是学习的前提；要安于寂寞，这是一种学习的心态；要持之以恒，这是学习的基础。要树立为中华民族崛起而学习的远大理想，并且为了实现理想锲而不舍、持之以恒、矢志不渝；要勤勤恳恳、踏踏实实，不游戏人生，不浪费时光；要淡泊明志，宁静致远，"板凳要坐十年冷，文章不写半句空"；不沽名钓誉、投机取巧、抄袭剽窃；敏而好学，不耻下问。

第三，你要主动尝试，锻炼自己做事的"本领"。

如果在大学只是通过书本学习知识，那是狭隘地接受大学教育，而提高能力和素质是大学教育中更为重要的内容。提高能力和素质的渠道是多种多样的，学校有学生会、科协等学生组织，还有各级各类学生社团，在保证学习的前提下，你们应该主动把握各种锻炼机会，多参加一些公益服务活动、专业竞赛和文体活动、社会实践和专业实习活动、人际交往和社团活动；也可以结合自己的兴趣爱好和专业，加入导师的科研团队。通过参加这些活动，扩大交友面，认识各类优秀的同学，收获真诚的友谊；培养自己的沟通和表达能力、领导和协调能力、实践和创新能力，发挥自身的兴趣特长，拓宽自己的发展视野，增强自己的综合素质，为将来的就业、创业和继续深造奠定基础。

同学们，大学生活是一本书，它的扉页已经揭开，我今天只为你们题写了序言，精彩的篇章还需要你们自己去书写和完成。希望你们在重大的每一天都因收获而快乐，因进步而幸福，让青春的花蕾带着美丽的梦想在这里傲然盛开，祝愿同学们人格健全、内心幸福、学习出彩！

从明天起同学们就要开始军训生活。新生参加军训是重大的光荣传统，你们要严格自律、听从指挥、服从命令，把部队的好思想、好作风学到手，留在学校；你们要尊重教官、虚心学习、刻苦训练、磨

砺品质。再过一个月，我们将迎来重庆大学建校 85 周年，希望你们通过这段时间的刻苦训练，以精彩的汇报表演献礼校庆 85 周年。

借此机会，我也代表学校向承接我校新生军训任务的部队官兵表示最诚挚的感谢和最崇高的敬意！预祝本次军训取得圆满成功！

谢谢大家！

Spiritual Qualities Required in Pursuit of Learning

—Speech at the Opening Ceremony of 2014 Graduate Students of Chongqing University

Dear students,

Good morning!

The fall ushers in the arrival of 4,700 new graduate students at home and abroad. On behalf of all the teachers and students of the university, I would like to extend a warm welcome to you for choosing Chongqing University for further study. I also congratulate you on opening a new chapter of your life from today. Research, exploration and innovation will become new themes of your campus life.

As an important part of higher education, graduate education is an important symbol to measure the level of higher education and the level and prospect of scientific, technological, economic and cultural development in a country. The development of graduate education has become a strategic choice for innovation-driven development and international competitiveness in countries around the world. The United States regards the graduate education system as a strategic resource of the country whose innovative ability and global competitiveness depend to a great extent on the strong graduate education system. European countries are committed to promoting the integration of European education with the help of the "Bologna Process". Japan has promulgated the *Graduate Education Revitalization Policy Outline*; and China, as a developing country, attaches great importance to the comprehensive reform and development of graduate education, which is regarded

做学问需要怎样的精神品质？

—— 在重庆大学 2014 级研究生开学典礼上的讲话

亲爱的同学们：

大家上午好！

金秋时节，重庆大学又迎来了海内外 4 700 名研究生新同学。首先，我代表学校全体师生员工对你们选择重大继续深造学习表示热烈的欢迎，也祝贺你们从今天起又一次开启了人生新的篇章，研究、探索和创新将成为你们校园生活新的主题。

研究生教育作为高等教育的重要组成部分，是衡量一个国家高等教育水平以及科技、经济、文化发展水平与前景的重要标志，发展研究生教育已成为世界各国创新驱动发展和提高国际竞争力的战略选择。美国把研究生教育体系作为国家的一项战略资源，其创新能力和全球竞争力很大程度上依赖于强大的研究生教育体系；欧洲各国借助于"博洛尼亚进程"，致力于推动欧洲教育一体化背景下的研究生教育改革；日本出台了《研究生教育振兴施策纲要》；我国作为发展中国家，更是高度重视研究生教育的综合改革与发展，把研究生教育作

Ministry of Education.

Students who will achieve master degrees should be masters of academic research. Academic research and study are your main tasks. But I have to say that study is a hard-creative process that requires a kind of spiritual support.

Firstly, you need to be innovative. Academic research is important in innovation. Innovation means breakthrough and leading, while non-innovation means falling behind. In recent days, the news of the first release of iPhone 6 is expected to have a "sting" for Chinese people, especially the "iPhone fans" are heartbroken. On the one hand, Apple factories in mainland China are processing and shipping goods to Chicago; on the other hand, Apple does not list mainland China among its first countries and regions to distribute iPhone 6.[1] Although we don't know if it is because Apple's marketing strategy or the license issue, in addition to the sadness for futility, we understand again that if we want to be independent, we must innovate independently; if we want to innovate independently, we must have high-level innovative talents. The lessons of history and the competition of reality tell us that innovation is the soul of national progress, and independent innovation is the premise of national independence. It can be said that all the graduate students here should become the new force of the national innovation force, should shoulder the responsibility of building an innovation-oriented country in the future, and represent the backbone of the national innovation system. You are strong, so innovation is; innovation is strong, so the country is! You have a great responsibility and a glorious mission. The hope of innovation rests on you.

Secondly, you need to study assiduously. Marx said, "There is no royal road to science, and only those who do not dread the fatiguing climb of its steep paths have a chance of gaining its luminous summits." Stories of ancients explain to us that assiduity counts in study. You must persevere in your studies. No matter what kind of research is done, it is not easy to get results and achieve success by just passing through, but a process of hard exploration. Darwin, Mendeleyev and other great scientists had studied painstakingly for decades, persevered with their research, and then gained remarkable achievements. A trickle of water can cut through stone after all, not because it is powerful, but because it drops day and night. In fact,

---

1   90% of Apple's suppliers and factories were located in China, but mainland China was not included in the first countries and regions where Apple launched its latest iPhone 6 on September 9, 2014.

和领先，不创新就意味着落后。最近几天，iPhone 6 首发的新闻估计对国人有所"刺痛"，尤其让"果粉"们伤心欲绝。一方面，位于中国内地的苹果代工厂正在抓紧加工出货并运往芝加哥；另一方面，苹果公司公布的上市国家和地区并无中国大陆[1]。虽然我们并不明白这是苹果公司的市场策略还是入网许可问题，除了免不了有一丝"为谁辛苦为谁忙"的伤感外，也让我们再次明白，想要自主市场，必须自主创新，想要自主创新，必须要有高层次的创新型人才。历史的教训和现实的竞争告诉我们，创新是民族进步的灵魂，自主创新是国家独立自主的前提。可以说，在座的各位研究生应该成为国家创新力量的生力军和后备军，肩负了未来建设创新型国家的重任，代表了国家未来创新体系的中坚力量。你们强，则创新强；创新强，则国家强！你们责任重大、使命光荣，创新的希望寄托在你们身上！

　　第二，需要有刻苦钻研精神。马克思说过，"在科学上没有平坦的大道，只有不畏劳苦沿着陡峭山路攀登的人，才有希望达到光辉的顶点"。古人悬梁刺股、凿壁偷光、囊萤映雪、负薪挂角的故事，都向我们说明了做学问需要有刻苦钻研精神。做学问要持之以恒。无论做什么研究，绝不是走马观花、浅尝辄止就能得到结果、取得成功的，都需要有一个艰苦探索的过程，达尔文、门捷列夫等大科学家都是苦心钻研几十年，坚韧不拔、锲而不舍，才取得了令人瞩目的成就。涓滴之水终究可以穿石，不是由于它力量强大，而是由于昼夜不停地滴坠。其实，失败距离成功只差一步，也许再走一步，失败就变成成功了。做学问需要点滴积累。荀子云："不积跬步，无以至千里；不积小流，无以成江海。"做学问必须有一个日积月累、循序渐进的过程，不能奢望一口吃个胖子，一夜成为大学者、大专家。日积月

1　苹果公司的供应商及工厂 90% 设在中国，但苹果公司于 2014 年 9 月 9 日推出最新款 iPhone 6 手机时，在首批上市国家和地区中，不包括中国大陆。

failure is only one step away from success; if you take another step, the failure will become a success. Study requires a little bit of accumulation. Xun Zi said, "Unless you pile up little steps, you can never journey a thousand li; unless you pile up tiny streams, you can never make a river or sea." Study must have a process of step-by-step accumulation like bees' gathering honey. According to some experts, a bee must collect pollen from one million flowers to make one kilogram of honey. In other words, only by "reading a million books" can you "write fluently". A man of research should concentrate on his studies. Some scholars say, "To learn, just like fighting on the battlefield, you have to fight without hesitation." Therefore, study should not be halfhearted and capricious; it is no use doing things without perseverance and the clear direction. If you run into problems, don't back down and don't relax. There is no royal road to study. Step by step, try to avoid being impetuous or eager to achieve. Plagiarizing others' achievements and falsifying experimental data are taboos in academic research. Research setbacks and failures are understandable and tolerated, while academic misconduct is not. Some people look for shortcuts to study, which is opportunistic, and ultimately unsuccessful and costly. This kind of lesson is too much and I hope you will resolutely resist academic misconduct in accordance with the rigorous academic attitude, follow the academic ethics formulated by the school, and carry forward the great academic style with the results of your hard work. Defend your own scholarship and defend your academic dignity and the reputation of the school.

Thirdly, you need to be critical. Innovation can't be separated from criticism, which is the source of innovation. The inventions and creations in the history of science and technology are inseparable from the critical spirit of scientists. By the end of the 19th century, physicists generally believed that physics had reached its peak and that great discoveries would never be made again. However, the discovery of roentgen rays and the Curies' discovery of radium revolutionized physics. Without Nicolaus Copernicus's critical spirit, natural science would not have been liberated from theology; without Feuerbach's critical spirit, there would be no selective inheritance of Hegelian philosophy, and Marxism would be difficult to appear. It is in criticism that mankind breaks through one forbidden zone after another, and then moves from the realm of necessity to the realm of freedom. The list goes on and on. The critical spirit is an indispensable factor in creative activities, which includes truth-seeking, questioning, self-confidence and curiosity, but the

累，才能厚积薄发，水滴石穿。做学问也像蜜蜂采蜜一样，据有关专家说，蜜蜂酿造一公斤蜜，必须在100万朵花上采集花粉。也就是说，只有"读书破万卷"，才能"下笔如有神"。做学问要专心致志。术业有专攻，学术贵在专一。有学者说，"做学问，就像战场上拼杀一样，要义无反顾"。因此，做学问不能三心二意、朝秦暮楚；一日曝十日寒，则读百年书，也难成大器。要一门深入，长期熏修；要明确方向，集中精力，几十年如一日，坐住冷板凳，下些笨功夫。碰到问题，不要退缩，咬定青山不放松，像螺丝钉一样，钉进去，钻到底。做学问不能投机取巧。要循序渐进，力戒心浮气躁，急于求成。抄袭、剽窃他人成果，伪造实验数据，是学术研究的大忌。研究上的挫折和失败是可以理解和宽容的，而学术上的不端行为是不能容忍的。有些人寻觅做学问的捷径，投机取巧，最终都是"偷鸡不成蚀把米"，"机关算尽太聪明，反算了卿卿性命"。这类教训太多、太深刻了，希望同学们本着严谨治学的态度，坚决抵制学术不端行为，遵循学校制定的学术道德规范，发扬重大的优良学风，用自己刻苦钻研、辛勤劳动的成果，去恪守自己的学者本分，捍卫自己的学术尊严和学校的声誉。

第三，需要有批判精神。创新离不开批判，批判是创新的源头活水。科技史上数以万计的发明创造，都离不开科学家的批判精神。19世纪末，物理学家们普遍认为，物理学已经发展到顶峰，伟大的发现不会再有。然而，伦琴射线的发现，居里夫妇的镭放射性发现，使物理学发生了巨大的革命。如果没有哥白尼的批判精神，自然科学就不会从神学中解放出来；如果没有费尔巴哈的批判精神，就没有对黑格尔哲学的扬弃，马克思主义也就难以登场。人类正是在批判中，突破了一个又一个禁区，才从"必然王国"走向了"自由王国"。类似的例子，在学术史上不胜枚举。在创造性活动中，批判性精神是不可缺

existence of critical spirit requires the independence of thought, personality and mind. As graduate students, you should strive to cultivate your own independent thinking, with courage to doubt authorities, curiosity to find the bottom of science, and confidence that none but "myself" can do it. Instead of a servile attitude to books, seniors, and foreign things, the scientific spirit of truth-seeking is the simply principle. Don't be conservative or lazy-minded. Do not follow what others say due to bigotry and arbitrary. In fact, the stumbling block on the road to progress is having no tolerance for any doubt about the tradition. Einstein also said, "It is often more important to ask a question than to solve it." In doing research work, one should not be superstitious about the existing conclusions, but should be good at discovering problems, dare to put forward questions, dare to expand new research fields and perspectives, and dare to question and correct the opinions, conclusions and methods of predecessors. When consulting the literature, don't be led by the opinions of the literature, and don't be bound by the existing conclusions. However, the critical spirit is not only to retain doubts and questions to others or the outside world, but also to scientifically examine, analyze and demonstrate one's own views and conclusions and strive to improve and enhance the thinking quality and master scientific innovation methods. In academic debates, we must respect the rights and personality of others and treat criticism equally.

Boys and girls, although the arduous road of research and innovation has a long way to go, as a new generation of intellectuals with pursuits and dreams, you must assume the heavy responsibility of evolving those "made in China" to be "created in China", which is also the value of your life. The graduate study period is the most brilliant and dazzling scene in life where you can enter the temple of scholarship, ascend to the heights of thought and science, peer into the mysteries of mankind and the universe, explore truth in research, discover reality in exploration, and grasp essence in innovation, which is not only an improvement on your study over ten years, but also a sublimation of your whole life. I wish you all the best in your youth!

Thank you!

少的因素，它包括求真、质疑、自信和好奇等；但批判精神的存在，需要思想、人格和精神的独立。研究生要努力培养自己独立思考、敢于怀疑的胆略，寻根究底的好奇心和舍我其谁的自信心，不畏惧权威、不唯书、不唯上、不唯洋、只唯真、只唯实的科学精神；不要因循守旧、思想懒惰、唯命是从、人云亦云、固执偏见、独断专行。其实，进步道路上的绊脚石，是不容许怀疑的传统。爱因斯坦也说："提出一个问题往往比解决一个问题更重要。"做研究工作，不要迷信已有的结论，要善于发现问题，敢于提出问题，敢于拓展新的研究领域和视角，敢于对前人的观点、结论、方法等提出质疑并予以修正。查阅文献时，不要做文献的"奴隶"，不要被文献的观点牵着鼻子跑，不要受现有结论所束缚。当然，批判精神不仅是对他人或外界保留怀疑和提问，也要对自己的观点、结论进行科学的审视、剖析和论证，努力改善和提高自己的思维素质，掌握科学的创新方法。在学术争论中，也要尊重他人的权利和人格，平等地对待批评和被批评。

　　同学们，尽管研究之路艰辛坎坷，创新之路任重道远，但作为有追求、有梦想的新一代知识分子，由"中国制造"实现"中国创造"的重任我们必须承载，这也正是我们人生的价值所在。研究生学习阶段，是人生中最灿烂、最耀眼的一幕。你们能够进入学术的圣殿，攀登思想和科学的巅峰，窥探人类和宇宙的奥妙，在研究中探究真理，在探索中发现真实，在创新中领悟真谛，这不仅是对前十几年学习的提升，更是对整个人生的升华。我衷心祝愿你们青春无悔！

　　谢谢大家！

Pass on CQU Spirit and Set Sail the Dream

—Speech at the Opening Ceremony of 2013 Undergraduates of Chongqing University

Dear students,

Good morning!

On the banks of the Huxi River, nestled between Gele Mountain and Jinyun Mountain, the beautiful Chongqing University campus welcomes 7,000 new students. On behalf of all the faculty and staff of the university and the senior students on campus, I would like to extend a warm welcome to you and congratulate you on your enrollment in Chongqing University!

From this day forward, you are formally on a journey to achieve your greatest ambitions. Here, you will spend the most memorable years in your life, comprehending the knowledge and learning skills of life and harvesting the most valuable friends in life. From now on, the beautiful mountain city is bound to be a haunting thought for your future or even in your life. Before the summer vacation, around the time you decided to apply for Chongqing University after the college entrance examination, I was very lucky to transfer from Lanzhou University to work at Chongqing University. You are my first students here, and I am destined to meet you in life, so I am as happy and excited as you are today. I am happy that "We are all freshmen!" and excited that I will work with you who are full of energy to create a better future for Chongqing University. With you, my mind will be young and happy! Thank you for choosing Chongqing University!

传承重大精神，梦想扬帆启程

—— 在重庆大学 2013 级本科生开学典礼上的讲话

亲爱的 2013 级全体新同学：

大家上午好！

歌乐巍巍，缙云婀娜，虎溪悠悠。在这两山环抱的虎溪河畔，隽秀美丽的重大校园又迎来了 7 000 名新同学。我谨代表学校全体教职员工和在校老生对你们的到来表示热烈的欢迎，祝贺你们成为新一代的重大人！

从今天开始，你们正式踏上了实现远大抱负的人生旅程。在这里，你们将度过生命里最为难忘的恬静岁月，领悟受用终身的知识与本领，也将收获人生中最为珍贵的挚友真情。从此，美丽山城注定成为你未来甚或此生都挥之不去的惦念。暑假前，大概就在你们高考后决定填报重庆大学的时候，我也非常幸运地从兰州大学调到重庆大学工作 [1]，你们是我在重大迎来的第一届新生，今生我和你们注定有缘。也正因为如此，今天我跟你们心情一样，十分高兴，无比激动。高兴

1 　周绪红于 2006 年 5 月—2013 年 6 月任兰州大学校长，2013 年 6 月—2017 年 12 月任重庆大学校长。

"985 Project". Today's Chongqing University has taken an international approach to open education and is moving towards a goal of being a distinctive, high-level university.

Chongqing University is a university of dreams. Since her establishment, we have been pursuing the dream of "building a great and profound university"[1] and have never stopped dreaming. Today, as a strategic center of China's higher education in the southwest, relying on the strategic advantages of the national "Project 985" and the regional advantages of Chongqing Municipality, we have established the connotative development path with the improvement of quality as the core, putting forward the goal of building a high-level university with characteristics, accelerating the construction of a modern socialist university system with Chinese characteristics, and establishing a pattern with the four mutually-supportive functions of personnel training, scientific research, social service and cultural transmission and innovation, and we are on the way of chasing the dream.

Chongqing University is a university of ideas. At the beginning of the school, a group of founders who returned after finishing overseas study introduced the advanced models of the world's modern universities to set up departments, design organizations and hire teachers. They also published the *Declaration of the Establishment of the Preparatory Committee of Chongqing University* and *Declaration of Chongqing University* and farsightedly put forward the idea of running a modern university— "riching scholarship, training talents, enlightening the country and the society". We pay great respect and just keep trying!

Chongqing University has always put education first, and has trained more than 200,000 highly qualified professionals for the country and society. We can say with pride, "Where there is construction, there are CQUers; where there is industry, there are CQUers." The CQUers have always been committed to rejuvenating the country through science and education, making important contributions to the scientific and technological progress of China. Chongqing University has always adhered to the school-running policy of "taking root in Chongqing, basing herself on the southwest, facing the west, serving the whole country and going to the world", starting from the needs of serving local economic and social development, timely adjusting the professional layout of disciplines, and making outstanding contributions

---

1   Quoted from *Declaration of Establishment of the Preparatory Committee of Chongqing University.*

年成为国家"985 工程"重点建设高校。今天的重庆大学，迈出了国际化的开放办学步伐，正朝着有特色、高水平大学的目标迈进。

重大是一所有梦想的大学。"建完备弘深之大学"[1]是自重庆大学成立之日起就不懈追求的梦想，为梦想我们不曾止步。今天的重大作为中国高等教育在西南的战略要地，依托国家"985 工程"的战略优势、重庆直辖市的地域优势，确立以提高质量为核心的内涵式发展道路，提出建设有特色、高水平大学的目标，加快建设中国特色社会主义现代大学制度，构建人才培养、科学研究、社会服务和文化传承创新四大功能相互支撑的格局，在追逐梦想的道路上正阔步前行。

重大是一所有理念的大学。建校伊始，一批留学归国的创办者就借鉴世界近代大学的先进模式，开办院系、设计组织、延聘师资，并且卓有远见地发布了《重庆大学筹备会成立宣言》和《重庆大学宣言》，前瞻未来地提出了"研究学术、造就人才、佑启乡邦、振导社会"的现代大学办学理念，蕴含着优秀的办学传统。令我们后人感慨、敬重不已，唯有只争朝夕，唯恐有辱使命！

重庆大学始终坚持育人为本，先后为国家和社会培养了 20 余万名高素质专门人才，历届毕业生已成为祖国建设各条战线的中坚力量。我们可以自豪地说："哪里有建设，哪里就有重大人；哪里有工业，哪里就有重大人。"历代重大人始终以科教兴国为己任，绘就了一幅幅艰苦创业、勇攀高峰的图强画卷，为新中国科学技术进步做出了重要贡献。重大始终坚持"扎根重庆，立足西南，面向西部，服务全国，走向世界"的办学方针，从服务地方经济社会发展的需要出发，及时调整学科专业布局，为国家和重庆市的经济、社会发展、生态文明建设做出了突出贡献。重大始终站在中国高等教育的前列，责无旁贷地肩负起建设有特色、高水平大学的历史使命，享有"嘉陵与

1　引自《重庆大学筹备会成立宣言》。

to the economic, social development and ecological civilization construction of Chongqing and the country as a whole. Standing at the forefront of China's higher education, Chongqing University is duty-bound to shoulder the historical mission of building a distinctive and high-level university, and has the reputation that "Jialing and the Yangtze River converge and produce Chongqing; the humanities and science have developed Chongqing University. "

Chongqing University is a university of great spirits. The history of Chongqing University is a history of perseverance, persistence and indomitable endeavor. In those uneven times, Chongqing University was born with difficulty; and its funding came from collecting the "pork tax" from farmers.[1] In the subsequent course of running the school, through the flames of war, after the adjustment of the departments, Chongqing University was on the verge of dissolution, experiencing twists and turns. During the War of Resistance Against Japanese Aggression, Chongqing University was in an important position in the southwest of China to save the nation from the War of Resistance. After the July 7th Incident of 1937, a large area of China fell under the Japanese aggressors. In order to analyze the situation of the War of Resistance and build up confidence that the War of Resistance will be won, Chongqing University which was in the southwest of the country twice invited Zhou Enlai to give a speech on the overall situation. In the war-torn environment of the time, Chongqing University, which was in trouble, extended its generous hands to the teachers and students of many famous universities of China such as Central University, Nankai University and Southeast University with a broad mind, and provided land and builded a campus for them. Chongqing University was born in a glorious land, integrating the spirit of the War of Resistance and the spirit of Hongyan. She has undergone the test of wars, inherited the ideal of Hongyan patriots, and cultivated countless literary talents. In the revolutionary struggle of national independence and liberation, a group of progressive teachers and students, such as Liu Guozhi[2] from Chongqing University, devoted themselves bravely and cast the eternal Hongyan spirit with their lives. Since the founding of

1   When serving as the first president of Chongqing University, Liu Xiang, who was the Commander of the No.21 National Revolutional Army and Chairman of Sichuan provincial government at that time, decided to add a dime of additional tax to the pork tax, which was expected to earn 150,000 yuan a year for running a school, thus solving the urgent need for the establishment of Chongqing University at that time.

2   Liu Guozhi (1921-1949) is the prototype of Liu Siyang in the classic red novel *Red Rock (Hongyan)*.

长江相汇而生重庆，人文与科学相济而衍重大"的美誉。

重大是一所有精神的大学。回溯重大的发展史，就是一部坚忍、执着、顽强的奋进史。在那风雨飘摇的年代，重庆大学的诞生举步维艰，其经费就是通过征收农民"猪肉税"[1]的办法来解决的。在随后的办学历程中，历战火纷飞，经院系调整，曾濒临解散，一波三折，置之死地而后生。在抗战年代，重庆大学与国家、民族同患难，挥起铁拳，捍卫河山，是西南地区抗战救亡的重要阵地。"七七事变"后，中国大片国土沦陷于日寇铁蹄之下。为了分析抗战形势，树立起抗战必胜的信心，身在西南一隅的重大学子两次邀请周恩来专门到重大作形势演讲。在当时的战乱环境里，患难之中的重庆大学以宽大的胸怀毅然向内迁至重庆的中央大学、南开大学、东南大学等诸多知名大学的师生伸出了慷慨的双手，提供土地、搭建校舍支持其办学。重庆大学诞生在光荣的土地上，融抗战精神、红岩精神于一体，经历了战争的考验、牺牲过红岩志士、生长出无数的文才义胆。在民族独立与解放的革命斗争中，重庆大学刘国锧[2]等一批进步师生英勇献身，用生命铸就了永恒的红岩精神。中华人民共和国成立后，重庆大学始终与国家同呼吸、共命运，与时代同前进。特别是改革开放以来，重庆大学以敢为人先的精神，大胆改革，不断实践，始终站在高等教育改革的前列，赢得了学校发展中的每一次重大机遇，发展成为国家高等教育格局中具有重要战略地位的一所大学。

八十多年栉风沐雨、励精图治，只要有希望，重大人就不曾让机遇错失；代代重大人踔厉前行、滋兰树蕙，锤炼出"耐劳苦、尚俭

---

1 重庆大学创办之初，国民革命军第 21 军军长兼四川省政府主席的刘湘兼任重庆大学第一任校长。为解决办学经费困难，刘湘决定在猪肉税中增加附加税一角，预计一年可以收入 15 万元用于办学，解了当时创办重庆大学的燃眉之急。

2 刘国锧（1921—1949），亦作刘国志，四川泸州人，红色经典小说《红岩》中刘思扬的原型。1947 年地下党组织建立沙磁特支，刘国锧任书记，具体领导重庆大学和沙磁区的革命斗争。

the People's Republic of China in 1949, Chongqing University has always shared the same destiny with the country and advanced with the times. Especially since the reform and opening-up policy, Chongqing University has always stood in the fore front of the higher education reform. She has won every great opportunity in the development of the university and developed into a university with an important strategic position in the pattern of national higher education.

For more than 80 years of concerted efforts and continued growth, Chongqing University people have never let the opportunity slip away as long as there is hope; generations of Chongqing University people work hard and forge the spirit of "Endurance, Frugality, Diligence, Patriotism"[1]. These words of Chongqing University's school motto are simple, low-key and pragmatic but have been inspiring generations of Chongqing University alumni like a spiritual totem for more than 80 years. Some people thought that it was "out of date", but it seems to me that its connotation is renewed throughout time.

"Endurance"(enduring toils) serves as the premise of bearing yourselves. Mencius said, " When Heaven is about to place a great responsibility on a great man, it always first frustrates his spirit and will, exhausts his muscles and bones, exposes him to starvation and poverty." There is no such thing as too much labor of strength and bones, but complex and diverse cultures, and impetuous utilitarianism will test you more than what you suffer from labor of strength. Although college life is colorful, there are various temptations lurking behind it. Enduring toils requires you to sharpen your mind and make it more mature in college. Maturity does not mean premature spirits nor sophistication, but a commitment to self-growth, the pursuit of ideals, immunity to the temptation of the outside world as well. The university is by no means a resting place after you have succeeded in squeezing through "the single-wood bridge", and it should be a new starting point for all of you.

"Frugality" plays as a style of life. Zhuge Liang said, "A man cultivates his moral character in peace and frugality. His aspiration cannot be clear if he tries to seek fame and wealth, nor he can reach the distant place if he is not in tranquility. " "Frugality" not only lies in the life frugality, but also lies in the inner peace and indifference to fame. Pursuing "frugality" is to ask you to be simple, abandon eager for quick success and instant benefit, not to flatter others and go after speculative gains, but adhere

---

1 The school motto of Chongqing University: Endurance, Frugality, Diligence, Patriotism.

朴、勤学业、爱国家"[1]的重大精神。重庆大学的这十二个字，朴素无华，低调务实，历经八十多年，如精神图腾般激励和影响着一代代重大人，成为重大精神文化的标志和根源。有人曾认为它"过时了"，而在我看来，其内涵历久弥新。

"耐劳苦"是做人、做事的前提。 孟子有云，"天将降大任于斯人也，必先苦其心志，劳其筋骨"。对于当今的你们而言，已没有太重的"筋骨之劳"，但在这个深刻变革、多元文化错综并呈、功利主义容易滋生浮躁的时代，比"劳其筋骨"更加考验你们的是"苦其心志"。大学生活固然五彩斑斓，但背后也潜伏着各种诱惑。"耐劳苦"，就是要求你们在大学里砥砺心志，使其更加成熟。"成熟"不是精神早衰，也不是世故圆滑，而是对自我成长的担当，对理想追求的执着，对外界诱惑的免疫。大学绝不是挤过独木桥后的休憩地，而应该成为你们策马扬鞭、继续前行的新起点。

"尚俭朴"是一种生活的格调。 诸葛亮曰"夫君子之行，静以修身，俭以养德。非淡泊无以明志，非宁静无以致远"。"俭朴"不仅在于生活节俭，更在于内心的宁静淡泊。"尚俭朴"，就是要求你们为人朴实，摒弃急功近利，不媚投机钻营，坚守诚信为本。"尚俭朴"，还希望你们志存高远，多一份理想主义情怀，有"望尽天涯路"的崇高追求，能耐得住"昨夜西风凋碧树"的清冷和"独上高楼"的寂寞，集中精力、静下心来读书。

"勤学业"是做学问的方法。 韩愈言"业精于勤，荒于嬉，毁于随"。大学四年犹如白驹过隙、稍纵即逝，你们应该珍惜时光，珍惜这来之不易的学习机会，充分利用好学校的优越环境多学习。不仅要学习知识本身，更要学习获取知识的能力；不仅要学好专业，而且要提高素养；不仅要学习理论，而且要学会实践；不仅要学习书本，而

---

1 "耐劳苦、尚俭朴、勤学业、爱国家"：重庆大学校训。

The day before yesterday, when I was welcoming the new students on the spot, several student reporters interviewed me with the same question: When the new students enter the university, what is the most important thing you want to say to them in a word as the president? I am here today to tell you that I hope you to know and love CQU, to study well, to cherish the time, and to continue the glorious chapters of CQU with your youth, and reflect the colorful light of CQU spirit through your wonderful lives!

You will start your military training tomorrow. It's a glorious tradition of CQU for new students to participate in military training. You should be strict in self-discipline, and obey the commands and orders. You should learn the good thoughts and style of the army. You must respect the instructors, learn with humility, train assiduously and hone your qualities. On behalf of the university, I would also like to take this opportunity to express our sincere thanks and highest respect to the officers and soldiers who will carry on our new students' military training! I wish this military training a complete success!

Thank you!

思想、好作风留在学校；你们要尊重教官、虚心学习、刻苦训练、磨砺品质。在这里，我也代表学校全体师生员工向此次承接我校新生军训任务的部队官兵表示衷心的感谢和崇高的敬意！预祝本次军训圆满成功！

　　谢谢大家！

How to Learn?

—Speech at the Opening Ceremony of 2013 Graduate Students of Chongqing University

Dear students,

Good morning!

In the first place, on behalf of all the teachers and students of Chongqing University, I would like to extend my warm welcome to you who have chosen Chongqing University for further study. I congratulate you on starting your glorious academic career today.

CQU boasts a history of 84 years. In 1948, famous professors Ke Zhao, Zhang Hongyuan and Feng Jian enrolled 11 graduate students, initiating graduate education in CQU. After the reform and opening-up, she has become one of the first institutions in China to award doctoral and master's degrees. Since June 2000, the development of graduate education in our school has turned a new page. At present, the number of graduate students has reached more than 18,500. In recent years, the graduate education of Chongqing University has adhered to the connotative development path with the core of improving the quality of training. A series of reforms have been carried out in aspects of stabilizing the scale, adjusting the structure, improving the quality of students, increasing the intensity of awards and assistance, strengthening the management of the training process, improving the tutor's responsibility mechanism, and establishing a monitoring system for the training quality; especially in the academic and professional graduate classification

怎样做学问？

——在重庆大学 2013 级研究生开学典礼上的讲话

亲爱的研究生新同学们：

大家上午好！

首先，我代表学校全体师生对你们选择重庆大学继续深造学习表示热烈的欢迎，也祝贺你们从今天起正式踏上了学术生涯的光荣征程。

重庆大学是一所有 84 年办学历史的大学，其研究生教育始于 1948 年，当年我校著名教授柯召、张洪沅、冯简招收 11 名研究生开创了重庆大学研究生教育事业的先河。改革开放后，重庆大学成为我国首批能够授予博士学位和硕士学位的单位之一。2000 年 6 月，教育部批准重大试办研究生院，从此重庆大学的研究生教育进入了一个新的跨越发展时期，目前在校研究生规模已达到 18 500 余人。近年来，重庆大学的研究生教育坚持走以提高培养质量为核心的内涵式发展道路，从稳定规模、调整结构、提高生源质量、加大奖助力度、加强培养过程管理、健全导师责任机制、建立培养质量监控体系等方面进行

living and studying in a superior environment, you should cherish the golden time and the hard-won opportunity, and make some achievements. If you don't cherish time, time will abandon you. I am confident that the knowledge you have acquired and the study methods you have developed during the graduate study will be of great benefit to your future achievements and your life.

The second is to be concentrated. Nothing can be done without concentration. The graduate study is no longer a complete reception of all kinds of novel and interesting knowledge, but it is necessary to learn to consciously develop yourself, select your own research direction under the guidance of the tutor in order to explore deeply and get somewhere with proficiency and focus. Being in-depth digging is the inevitable requirement of innovation. You should spot a focus on elective courses, literature review, research practice, experimental research and other aspects instead of hitting and missing. This is like a magnifying glass that can ignite the blazing flame only when the scattered sunlight is concentrated. Nothing can be accomplished without a definite direction. In other words, we should concentrate on study. But this is a difficult process. It requires strong perseverance and extraordinary courage. We should carefully consider the school motto of "Endurance, Frugality, Diligence, Patriotism", which was put forward at the beginning of the establishment. It promotes unpretentious and down-to-earth attitudes, and is particularly precious in today's social environment. Marx also said, "There is no royal road to science, and only those who do not dread the fatiguing climb of its steep paths have a chance of gaining its luminous summits."

The third is to be rigorous. Rigorous scholarship is an academic quality that every graduate student must possess. Academic integrity has become a concern in society, which has seriously affected the credibility of academic achievements. The title of "expert" has become a public joke, which is the tragedy of academia. Down the road, you may become designers holding drawings, analysts alongside test tubes, or judges pounding gavels, or public figures holding microphones ... No matter what you do, please remember that your integrity can be the positive and dishonesty the negative. Without integrity, you will lose your dignity. The consciousness of integrity comes from the rigorous scholarship in study: treating scientific research with a rigorous attitude, reflecting scientific processes with real data, and insisting on the scientific research style of seeking truth from facts. Anyone who violates the ethics of scientific research will pay a heavy price for it. We must have a serious scientific attitude and

龄。你们正处于人一生中精力最充沛、思维最活跃、最具创造力的时期，并且处于一个优越的生活和学习环境里，理应珍惜美好时光，珍惜这来之不易的深造机会，有所创造、有所成就。抛弃时间的人，时间就会抛弃你；莫等闲，白了少年头，空悲切！我相信，你们在研究生阶段获取的知识、形成的学习方法，将有益于你们未来取得杰出的成就，受用终身。

二是要集中精力。凡事聚精会神，方有所成。研究生阶段不再是对各种新奇有趣知识的"全盘接收"，而要学会有意识地向纵深"开发"自己，在导师的指导下选准自己的研究方向，精诚专一，深入探讨，才能学有成就。"深入"是创新的必然要求，选修课程、查阅文献、调研实践、试验研究等各个环节都应该有一个关注的焦点，而不能再像大学阶段那般"漫无边际"。这就像放大镜一样，只有把分散的阳光集中起来，才能燃起熊熊的火焰。没有确定的方向，朝三暮四或者三心二意，则将一事无成。也就是说，要集中精力、沉下心来做学问。但这是一个艰辛困苦的过程，需要坚强的毅力和过人的勇气，必须吃得了苦，耐得了寂寞。我们要仔细体味重大在创办之初就提出的"耐劳苦、尚俭朴、勤学业、爱国家"的校训，它推崇朴实无华、脚踏实地，在当今稍显浮华功利的社会环境下，显得尤为珍贵。马克思也说过："在科学上没有平坦的大道，只有不畏劳苦沿着陡峭山路攀登的人，才有希望达到光辉的顶点。"

三是要严谨治学。严谨治学是每一位研究生必须具备的学术品质。学术诚信已成为当今社会关注的重要话题，已严重影响到学术的公信力。"专家"称谓沦为大众的调侃和笑谈，不能不说是学术界的悲哀。今后，大家可能手握图纸成为一名设计师，或者手握试管成为一名分析师，或者手握法槌成为一名法官，或者手握话筒成为一名公众人物……无论你做什么，请记住你的一言一行诚信与否，都可能成

a high sense of responsibility, abide by scientific ethics and academic norms, and consciously maintain a healthy academic environment.

The forth is to be united. Unity and cooperation are the important bases for prosperity of our scientific research. Everyone's knowledge and ability are limited, and it is impossible for anyone to develop "comprehensively" in an absolute sense. We are not traditional farmers single-handed from sowing to reaping. We are adrift Robinsons who get somewhere only with others' helping hands. Individuals cannot undertake major national research projects, and it is difficult to train large numbers of talents and to improve the innovation ability and form the competitive power of science and technology. We must learn to cooperate and compete in the training of "lab team" and "tutor team", learn to obey and lead, and learn to deal with the relationship between individuals and tutors, the relationship between personal interests and team orientations, and learn to cultivate the sense of teamwork, and learn to grow together with tutors and classmates. We must develop good psychological quality, adjust all aspects of pressure, and face challenges that may be encountered with a healthy attitude.

Dear students, when most of your peers have begun to accumulate experience and build careers, you are willing to be poor and choose to continue your studies in Chongqing University, showing your determination not to settle for mediocrity. I believe that with the cultivation of Chongqing University and your personal efforts, you will certainly be able to better display your talents to realize the value of life, and return the country on a broader stage.

Finally, I wish all of you have a happy life and success in your studies at Chongqing University!

Thank you!

为时代正反两个方向的推手。没有诚信，你将失去尊严。诚信意识从何而来，要从学习阶段的严谨治学开始做起。以严谨的态度对待科学研究，用真实的数据反映科学过程，坚持实事求是的科研作风。任何违背科研伦理的人，都要为此付出沉重的代价。大家务必要有严谨认真的科学态度和高度的责任感，恪守科学道德和学术规范，自觉维护健康的学术环境。

四是要团结协作。团结协作是我们科研事业兴旺发达的重要基础。每个人的知识和能力是有限的，任何人都不可能在绝对意义上"全面"发展。我们不是传统的农民，从播种到收获，单枪匹马。我们就像漂流的鲁滨逊一样，只有同别人在一起，才能完成许多事业。散兵游勇、单干户、父子兵、小作坊的研究方式，无法承担国家重大科研项目，难以培养"将才""帅才"和大批人才，难以提高科技创新能力和形成竞争实力。我们要在"实验室团队""导师团队"的训练中，学会合作与竞争，学会服从与领导，处理好个人与导师、个人兴趣与团队方向的关系，培养团队协作意识，学会与导师和同学们共同成长。我们要养成良好的心理素质，调节好各方面的压力，以健康的心态面对可能遇到的挑战。

同学们，在多数同龄人都已开始在社会上积累经验、开创事业的时候，你们却甘于清贫，选择在重大继续深造，显示了你们不甘平凡、追求卓越的决心。我相信，有重大的培养再加上你们个人的努力，你们一定不会辜负这份决心，必定会为自己今后更好地施展才华、实现人生价值、回报国家获得更宽阔的舞台。

最后，祝愿大家在重庆大学学习、生活愉快，学有所成！

谢谢大家！

Postscript

"We are common people coming from plain worlds. But as long as we work hard in our own world and do every ordinary thing around us well, we are successful! Bosom in plainness, dream in common!" The value passed by President Zhou Xuhong is that young people can pinpoint themselves in plainness and that more people can understand the value of ordinary life in this era.

Once upon a time, people like to dub college students "God's favored ones". However, the community, which could never be an ivory tower, demands everyone to chase the wheel of the times. Today, when the devision of labor is more diverse, cultures more plural and social contradictions more complex, various opportunities and challenges are facing everyone. However, life has a length and getting a niche in society is only a starting point. If you cannot pinpoint yourselves with down-to-earth efforts, then you will probably fail the opportunities given by this era on your journey.

As Lu Yao said in *World of Plainness*, "Everyone's life is also a world. Even the most plain one has to fight for the existence of his world." The years from the mid-1970s to the mid-1980 under his pen was a turbulent period encountering a historical transformation, when chronic material deprivation implanted a deep sense of hunger in people's minds, and the reform of land ownership allowed young people to see dreams and believe that they could realize their self-worth even in an ordinary life. The positive values the "world of plainness" conveyed have greatly inspired a generation.

Now, young people are in a new period of historical transition. With China's

后　记

　　"我们都是平凡人，因为我们都来自'平凡的世界'；但我们都可以成功，只要我们在自己的世界里尽力去奋斗，把身边每一件平凡的事做好，你就是成功的人！尽管你身处平凡，但在平凡的世界里一定会有人懂你！"周绪红校长传递的价值观，是希望年轻人能在平凡的世界中找到自我，是希望这个时代能有更多人懂得平凡人生的价值。

　　曾几何时，说起大学生，人们最喜欢用"天之骄子"来形容。但是，社会不是象牙塔，每个人都必须跟着时代车轮滚滚向前。在今天，社会分工更为多样，社会文化更加多元，社会矛盾也更加复杂，每个年轻人都在面对着种种机会，也在面临着种种挑战，而人生是有长度的，从某种意义讲，踏入社会只是一个起点。如果不能清晰地找准自己的定位，不能在仰望星空的时候将双脚坚实踩在大地之上，那么，在人生征途上就很可能辜负这个时代赋予的机遇。

　　诚如路遥在《平凡的世界》里所说，"每个人的生活同样也是一个世界。即使最平凡的人，也得要为他那个世界的存在而战斗"。路遥笔下的年代，是 20 世纪 70 年代中期至 80 年代中期，那是一个历史转型的震荡年代，长期的物质匮乏在人们心中植入了深刻的饥饿感，而土地所有制改革让年轻人看到梦想，相信平凡的人生也可以实

译者序

　　高校的立身之本在于立德树人，需要坚持将思想政治工作贯穿教育教学全过程，实现全员育人、全程育人、全方位育人。

　　大学校长的开学典礼与毕业典礼讲话是大学生思想政治教育的重要环节，在泛介质传播背景下，对其关注与广泛传播具有普适性教育价值。开学典礼通常作为大学新生的"第一课"，既是新生入学教育的"开场白"，也是新生开启接受高等教育的"成人礼"。毕业典礼中的校长讲话被誉为大学生在校期间的"最后一堂课"，校长讲话承载着母校对毕业生的寄望与期盼，具有重要的育人功能。大学校长的讲话对大学生明确学习方向、感悟高校文化、体会大学精神、激发成长动力、实现人生转折具有重要指导意义，同时是高校展示与表达高等教育理念，挖潜"立德树人"教育内涵，阐述"培养什么人？怎样培养人？为谁培养人？"的重要契机，体现教育理念的时代性与传承性，承载着重要的教育功能和育人使命，映射着大学办学理念和精神文化。《平凡的世界会有人懂你》是重庆大学校长周绪红院士在任期间，对当代大学生的"时代精神""理想信念""价值塑造""生涯规划"等问题的诠释。

　　在网页上搜索国外大学校长的讲话，译著、视频、音频、文章等不胜枚举，其中不乏中英双语版，但反观中国大学校长讲话的英文版却寥寥无几。译者翻译此书的目的是使国外读者了解中国高等教育理念与中国学者的担当与使命。

翻译源于对原文本的深刻领悟。研究校长讲话话语风格意蕴，是源于译者对原作语言风格的认同和喜爱，翻译内容从本质上体现了高等教育对中国特色社会主义道路自信、理论自信、制度自信、文化自信的高度认同和践行。《平凡的世界会有人懂你》凸显中国语言特色，以融通、理性、多元视角打造具有中国风格的高等教育话语体系。以通达自如的语言展现对高等教育的感悟和高度概括；以传播主体和受众主体的交流互动强化高等教育情感认同；在术语、修辞、话语、叙事等多种语言层面升华语言审美情趣、审美个性和审美形态。

译者力求在阅读和理解原文本过程中，兼顾语言认知与美感体验双重作用，通过双重活动认识理解原文，并在大脑中形成格式塔意象，再用译文语言将此意象再造，在阅读、理解、再造等中介活动中再塑原作美感，实现原文内涵的有效转换和再现。译者团队在翻译过程中，着重于中国特色术语、修辞与篇章等层面：（一）对文中中华传统文化特色词的翻译，如俗语、典雅语、古语词、外来词、新词、网络用语、熟语等参考"当代中国特色话语外译传播平台""中国特色话语对外翻译标准化术语库""新时代中国特色话语大数据平台"等多个数据平台，力求术语翻译的规范与统一；（二）对文中所引用的中华优秀古典诗词的翻译，在理解原诗、形成意象、模糊表述的认知选择过程中，充分运用语义模糊、语法模糊及意象模糊策略，使译作达致动态的、模糊的、有机的对等；（三）对文中句式结构、语义推进、句子省略的翻译，关切排比句句式转换，保持原著画面感，重塑从近处推向远处，从当前现实摇向深邃历史的"读者期待"表述逻辑。

译者翻译时遵循的首要原则便是忠实于原文。风格作为原文不可分割的一部分，译者在翻译时力求在译入语中再现原文的风格且使译文符合目标语读者的阅读习惯。因此译者秉持传达原作"风趣"格致，保留原作表述口吻，译法上趋向灵活处理，不硬译并适当添加注解。

译稿经过三译三改三校，历时两年完成。成书过程中有幸得到原作者周绪红校长的悉心指导，重庆大学出版社编辑的大力支持，外方校译的积极努力及翻译团队的通力合作，在此深表谢意！

译无止境，译文错漏浅薄之处，祈请读者朋友不吝赐教，以利再版时修订和完善。

单宇

2023 年 1 月于长沙

图书在版编目（CIP）数据

平凡的世界会有人懂你：周绪红任重庆大学校长期
间寄语新生和毕业生：汉英双语版 / 周绪红著；单宇
译 . -- 重庆：重庆大学出版社，2023.2

ISBN 978-7-5689-3400-8

Ⅰ . ①平… Ⅱ . ①周… ②单… Ⅲ . ①演讲 - 中国 -
当代 - 选集 - 汉、英 Ⅳ . ① I267

中国版本图书馆 CIP 数据核字 (2022) 第 117681 号

平凡的世界会有人懂你
周绪红任重庆大学校长期间寄语新生和毕业生（汉英双语版）
PINGFAN DE SHIJIE HUI YOUREN DONGNI
ZHOUXUHONG REN CHONGQING DAXUE XIAOZHANG QIJIAN JIYU XINSHENG HE BIYESHENG

周绪红 著

单 宇 译

责任编辑：杨 琪 版式设计：周安迪
责任校对：王 倩 责任印制：赵 晟
*
重庆大学出版社出版发行
出版人：饶帮华
社址：重庆市沙坪坝区大学城西路 21 号
邮编：401331
电话：（023）88617190 88617185（中小学）
传真：（023）88617186 88617166
网址：http://www.cqup.com.cn
邮箱：fxk@cqup.com.cn（营销中心）
全国新华书店经销
重庆升光电力印务有限公司印刷
*
开本：720mm × 960mm 1/16 印张：12.75 字数：197 千
2023 年 2 月第 1 版 2023 年 2 月第 1 次印刷
ISBN 978-7-5689-3400-8 定价：69.00 元